ALT-ERNATE

A Collection of 37 Stories

MELANIE HARDING-SHAW

For me…

… and also, for you.

CONTENTS

INTRODUCTION

Five years ago, on the 9th of April 2016 when my children were six, four, and two, I sat down and decided to write a middle-grade high fantasy novel. The last time I had written fiction would have been sixth-form English when I was sixteen. My husband was a screenwriter when we met, but I'd never had the energy or inclination to extend beyond writing the policy briefings and cabinet papers of my day job. That night, I wrote my first 685 words and over the next 18 months I wrote 64,000.

In February 2018, I started writing short stories and I wasn't just writing for my kids anymore. At some point I started calling myself a writer even though it felt like I was pretending. I had stories accepted into magazines and anthologies. I set up a website. I found the most amazingly supportive group of writing friends I could ever wish for and I found myself. It was an alternate self I desperately needed that was entirely separate from being Mel the mum or Mel the bureaucrat.

The first two sentences I wrote back in 2016 were these: *Curiosity flew above the shipyard of Anderah leaning into the warm thermals rising from below. The people working on the ground, tiny in the distance, took no notice.* It's easy to forget how high we've managed to soar and to feel like no one will notice. I rack up well over 100 story rejections every year. Last year, I burned out and wrote nothing at all for months on end. Sometimes it feels like nothing will ever happen again.

This book is my reminder that things have happened and that they will continue to happen. It is my reminder that writing is joy; that my brain loves to drift through alternating genres, ideas, and lengths and twist them up into stories I didn't know were hovering in my consciousness. I've written over 300,000 words over the last five years. It's not much for some, but it's a lot more than the zero I'd written before that and it's a lot less than I will have written in another five or fifteen years.

This collection includes a story for each year of my life so far, alternating between micro-fiction and longer stories and including five previously unpublished works to celebrate my fifth anniversary of writing. The stories are fantasy, science fiction, slipstream and horror. They've been published in over 20 different publications. They range from sweet or light-hearted to downright dark, but even in the sweet there is always a hint of the creepy, strange or melancholy.

Alt-ernate is a window to the alternate me that has been growing since 2016. I hope you enjoy the view. Thank you for your support.

AN AVIAN INTRODUCTION

First published in *GeyserCon Book* in May 2019.

There are places where the boundaries are thin and a step off the path could take you further than you meant to go. There are three kinds of travellers there – those, like most of us, who never notice the rent in the veil; those who take that step and wander lost forever; and a very few who return carrying the ethereal boundary with them to become a nexus of fragile reality walking the earth.

Anna had a pouch of scroggin hooked on her belt, a friend lifting her pack from behind to take the weight off her shoulders, and the alluring memory of a painting of the Pink and White Terraces from a dimly-lit art auction drawing her on.

Kōkako had the nearby flowering flax for energy, a careless ponga that had lost its top to perch on, and the songs of her family echoing across Lake Rotomahana calling her to fly.

Anna's right heel was forming a blister. The path seemed to go on forever. Her curious eyes wandered, searching for the origins of the birdsong riding the breeze.

Kōkako's wings ached to stretch free. The air currents played before her. Her joyous cascade of chirrups burst forth, telling the story of layers of reality hiding beneath the trees.

Anna gasped as a view of the lake opened up before her. She watched a tiny green shape flitting from a ponga, down towards the water and then back upwards to the safety of the bush.

Kōkako felt the eyes watching. Maybe this time they would see. She twisted through the rift Mount Tarawera had torn all those years ago, flew high above terraced pools glinting in the sunshine, and then back down to the place between.

Anna blinked.

Kōkako waited.

There are guides who mean you well even as they lead you astray and there are guides who act for their own designs. A portal goes both ways. When you carry those ethereal boundaries with you, new fissures open in places they were never meant to be—supermarkets, libraries, the streets of nearby Rotorua. The past is not the only place they will take you and you are not the only thing that will travel between.

What follows you home will not be New Zealand's first invasive species.

STRANDS OF OUR TOMORROWS

First published in *The Arcanist* in August 2019.

They say your hair keeps growing after you die, but it isn't true. It's just your skin shrinking away from long-dead cells as if dissociation might somehow undo death. Most people have over 100,000 hairs on their head. The day she left me, I only asked for a lock. If I'd asked for more she would have said no. She gave me 157 strands.

They were dark, glossy brown and the same length as the line from the inside of my knee to the top of my inner thigh that she used to trace with her kisses. She was used to my strange requests and it wasn't until she was holding the lock out to me that she hesitated. I think she would have asked why, but the tears were rolling down my cheeks. Instead, she just let me take it.

We were camped by a river surrounded by weeping willows with draping branches that screened her from my view as she walked away. My pain radiated out to my breasts and down my body, fusing me to the ground. My tears rolled down to the river, making it swell in its banks. The wind whipped the branches of the willows across my face. They tangled with my hair until it was impossible to tell where the tree ended and I began.

I came to my senses when I smelled springtime — ducklings, sweet hyacinths, and friendlier rain. I reached into my pocket for her lock of hair and drew out a single strand. I tore my own hair from the grasp of the willow and knelt down to dig into the damp earth. I planted that single strand in the ground; that strand as long as my lap where she would lay like a newly born baby with the shape of an adult woman. When the hair was safely nestled in the earth, I watered it with my tears and blew springtime's breath into her growing lungs.

She grew quickly, her body racing to match the age of the hair it seeded from. Soon I had a companion again, but that growth does not slow. She reached the years we had been together in the blink of an eye and before I knew it, I was watching her walk away. My heart breaking all over again.

I tried all the different seasons' breaths (except winter, of course, I wouldn't waste a precious strand like that). But in the end, she always left. Finally, I reached into my pocket and a single strand met my touch. The last one. Even as she grew before me, I felt the pain of her leaving start.

This time, when she pushed the willow branches aside to leave me, I called out "May I come with you?"

She stared at me for a long moment, one eye slightly wider than the other in that look she always gave me when I was being 'other' and then she nodded.

We travelled to the city together, not touching. I could feel my pain wrapping around us, pulling me forward. When we got to the hospital my companion started to look confused. When we got to the room she stopped in the doorway and began to cry.

I walked to the bed and looked down at my lover. Her hair was white and her skin was wrinkled from a lifetime I had not been there to see. She didn't have much time left. Her eyes were fading, but they widened all the same when she looked at my face.

"You look just like when I left you by the river," she said. I sat down and held her dry textured hand in mine.

My last companion — number 157 — stepped into the room and stood by the bed. She was only weeks from this state herself but I had never been there to see it before. Right now, she looked just like my lover did when she walked away 50 years ago. She sat down and held my lover's other hand.

The old woman looked at me with one eye slightly wider than other and tears tracing down the streambeds of her wrinkled cheeks. "Is she like you? Will she live forever?"

I shook my head and my companion looked confused again.

"May I have another lock of your hair?" I asked, and I saw my lover start to understand. She shrank away from me and my companion then, pulling her hands away as if that dissociation might change the reality sitting before her.

We stayed like that for a long time before she responded. The gap between each of her breaths growing longer and longer.

"No, my love. Find something else to grow," she said.

Her breath became ragged and then silence fell as I watched her life slip away from her.

My tears poured down to the floor and flooded the hallways. I leaned forward and kissed her lips while they were still warm, blowing winter's breath into her old lungs. Her body stayed motionless and quickly cooling, but her white hair grew so long it filled the room, filled the hospital, and carried me out of its doors into the sunshine cradled in the strands of her death.

When it finally stopped, it spilled me out onto the road. I knelt on the rough asphalt and watched my tears spread as sheets of water to fall down the drains nearby. I don't know how long I knelt like that. It could have been a minute, a day, a season, a year.

"Are you OK?" a voice asked from behind me.

I turned to face the sound. My eyes traced up black skinny jeans and a loose singlet to a face framed in flowing red hair. My breath caught.

"Maybe," I said and the woman smiled.

I was more prepared this time, it only took me a week to convince her. The hairdresser gave me the ponytail as she cut it from her locks — 100,000 strands.

LOVE NOTE

First published in *Takahē* in April 2020.

I had forgotten how the harbour's waters speak the mood of Wellington. Static, sparkling cerulean. Violent, murky brown. Capped in trembling froth like a vast flat-white with the wind just another stimulant to the city's residents.

When you have been away from a city and return, it can feel like you are a stranger. Ethereal urban landmarks disappear to be replaced by glass and steel, twinkling laneways and rainbow tar seal. The foundations remain though. A city reclaimed from the ocean, built on creativity and public service.

I'm sure you can see my nostalgia runs deep. We did not part on the best of terms. I hope you understand I never meant to hurt you. I, of all people, understand when life's pressures grow too much to bear, or even just too much to bare.

You stood in voiceless condemnation when I left and I thought perhaps this time would be different. Perhaps this time I would stay away. But, the fissures of past pain draw me back every time. It wasn't all bad, was it? Was there a time your trembling was not fear?

Alt-ernate – Melanie Harding-Shaw

I used to think I changed you when I broke you.
When my actions left you crumpled. I saw your scars
and thought I had marked you as my own. I know
different now. Your scars do not define you.
Windswept waters still sparkle in the sun. Creativity
and service shine even brighter in the wake of my
destruction.

Your foundations go deep, but not into the earth.
All my love,
Kēkerengū Fault

A DEVOTED HUSBAND

First published in *Breach Zine* in November 2018.
Finalist, Best Short Story, Sir Julius Vogel Awards

"Silver lining is definitely one of our most popular. An excellent choice," Madam Lutien said. The customer's hands shook a little as she took the package from her and hurried out of the dim shop. Business was always good in winter. It had to keep them going for the rest of the year.

Belle, the shop assistant, restocked the shelves throughout the day—silver lining, nostalgia, opportunism. At midday they received a Government batch-order for impartiality.

"We're running low on devotion," Belle called to the Madam as she re-checked the shelves.

In the mornings Mr Lutien harvested the stock. In the afternoons, he minded the store-front while Madam Lutien tended the orchard. Every day he brought her a carefully constructed bacon and avocado croissant made just the way she liked it and a cup of strong black tea. It had been thoughtful the first time.

The Madam had taken to checking the accounts as she ate. Mr Lutien would hover nearby waiting for some sign of approval, hands clasped before him, hazel eyes locked on her. She pretended not to notice. Each day the ledger moved a little further into the red. Madam Lutien couldn't bring herself to care. She was tired of being tied to this place.

When the shop was built, it had been on the edge of the city. Madam Lutien's forebears had fenced a paddock behind it and planted thirty-seven matte-black twisted trunks that formed a spiral path. The city had long since swallowed both shop and orchard. Where fences had once bounded the paddock, there were now three-storey blank concrete walls on all sides. It hadn't even occurred to the neighbours to put windows on those walls. No-one wanted to see what grew there. Generations of Madam Lutien's family had tended the trees and sold their fruit according to strict traditions passed from mother to daughter.

Madam Lutien shivered a little in the winter chill as she made her way out the back door of the shop. The shaded orchard was only marginally brighter than the store's dim interior. Each black trunk was covered in spiny branches that crept outwards over the path. The fruits of those branches were eyeballs. As Madam Lutien stepped onto the orchard path, hundreds of eyes turned to track her movements. Irises of blue, brown, green, hazel, grey and all the shades in between nestled in heavily bloodshot white globes all around her. There were no eyelids to protect them and no tear ducts to wash the dust away.

Madam Lutien cursed as she felt a wet popping underneath her foot. An over-ripe eyeball had fallen to the ground. Mr Lutien was becoming a problem. He didn't have the affinity needed to assess when the stock was ready. Her mother had tried to warn her. But who listened to their mother's opinion on such things? Now her mother was gone and it was her job to keep the family business afloat.

The undertakers had delivered a new set of bodies, carefully tagged with personality profiles and left in silver-lined boxes along the walls. She checked the profiles and then wheelbarrowed each body to the appropriate trunk. She watched as black roots twisted up out of the ground to encase the latest acquisitions and suck them into the earth. A lifetime of watching the orchard meant she could identify when a neighbouring tree's roots were trying to snatch the wrong body away. A sharp jab with a silver poker made the roots snap back into the ground. None of the latest deliveries were going to fill their shortfall of devotion.

Once all the bodies had been absorbed, she wandered the spiral path misting water onto the reddest eye-globes. The customers found overly-bloodshot eyes challenging. She carried secateurs on her belt and ensured every stray branch she passed was cut right back. The trees were constantly testing boundaries and had to be kept ruthlessly under control, much like an elaborate topiary garden.

Her wandering took her to a bench in the very centre of the spiral next to a stunted trunk that barely reached her waist. It was blacker than any other tree here. Its eyeballs alone were often discarded unsold. There was a place for every product, but some must be treated with caution.

The Madam stood there for a long time thinking and remembering. The sun was setting by the time she reached out and pulled an eyeball with a crystal-clear blue iris from the stunted trunk. It wasn't quite ripe. Its effects shouldn't last long. Before she could rethink, she put it into her mouth and bit down until she felt the soft explosion that filled her mouth with sour vitreous fluid.

She'd forgotten how intoxicating the rush of feeling was. Her eyes dilated and she slumped back onto the bench letting the sensation overwhelm her. That was how Mr Lutien found her 30 minutes later, although he mistook her intoxication for despair.

"Come, my love. You'll feel better after I make you some dinner."

He pulled her to her feet and led the way back out of the spiral path. Madam Lutien pulled them to a stop by the bare devotion tree. The hungry roots were starting to pop out of the ground like garden eels;

finger-length undulating tendrils waving back and forth. She crouched down to look closer, wondering how long they had before the tree took matters into its own 'hands'.

"Come away from there Alice, it's not safe," Mr Lutien called uneasily. He came to stand next to her and put a hand on her shoulder.

Madam Lutien didn't move. All she could see of her husband was his black gumboots standing next to her. She watched with curious detachment as a waving black tendril popped up just behind them. For a moment she tried to remember how that should make her feel. Then she let the cold rush of intoxicating detachment wash over her again.

She put a hand out to catch herself as the ground lurched around her. The soil vibrated under her fingers. She felt something caress her palm where it was pressed flat against the ground. Mr Lutien's hand left her shoulder. She closed her eyes and wondered what all the noise was.

When she opened them again, she stood and collected a pair of empty black gumboots from beside her. She looked at the tree before her and traced her finger over the many new buds that had formed along the nearest branch; far more that would usually grow from a single dead body. Most of them would take a week or more to mature, but two were growing much faster – one near her and one high above facing up to the sky. She watched as they swelled and bulged in their black casing, pulling back and forth as the fruit struggled to break free.

A tiny crack appeared at the bottom of the globe nearest her and spread upwards. Madam Lutien reached out and carefully peeled the casing away. A familiar hazel eyeball stared back at her, the pupil so dilated that the colour was just a thin halo. The thrill of artificial detachment was starting to fade and she imagined she could see accusation and betrayal in its depths.

She shifted her weight from foot to foot and the eyeball waved back and forth tracking her movements, locked on her. Madam Lutien frowned in annoyance; that wouldn't do. She reached out, plucked the ripe eye from the tree, and popped it in her mouth before she could rethink.

Warmth radiated through her body from the eye settling in her stomach. For a minute she felt the warmth fighting with the artificial viewpoint already coursing through her. Then the two flavours seemed to find an equilibrium. She pushed aside a memory of her grandmother warning her against mixing the stock and looked around herself with burgeoning enthusiasm.

The dedication she had felt when she first took over the family business was returning. She was sure she could get them back in the black. The answer was volume. She needed to branch out and explore new supply chains for the bodies that fed the trees. She stared at the multitude of buds on the tree in front of her, three or four bodies worth. It was so much more efficient. Once production was up she could reduce the pruning schedule so the harvest was larger. There was no point sticking to her family's strict rules if it meant the business died.

She felt a single drop of water fall on her lip as she turned away. She looked up in surprise at the cloudless sky. All she could see above her were the twisting bare branches of the devotion tree and the single ripe eyeball staring upwards. She licked her lip and tasted salt.

She was so deep in thought as she returned to the house that she didn't even notice she was still holding the empty black gumboots until she was standing in the study. Just like she hadn't noticed the devotion tree reaching its branches wider and higher than it ever had before.

The next week the shop was busy and Madam Lutien was heading out to meet a bank manager about expanding the business.

"I'm sorry Sir, we're running low on Devotion. Can I interest you in a Sanguine?" the shop assistant Belle said to a gentleman in a trench coat and trilby.

"I harvested some fresh Devotion last night Belle," Madam Lutien called over her shoulder.

Her eyes looked far into the distance as she stepped out the door. Her mind was full of plans to grow the orchard, devoted to its propagation. Beside her feet, unnoticed, a single undulating black tendril was peeking through the cracked concrete steps that led into the city.

SHE WAS NO WITCH

First published in *Curses & Cauldrons* from Blood
Song Books in August 2019

They called her witch in whispers thinking she would
not hear. Nothing made her madder. She was no
witch. She had no healing potions to misunderstand.
No jealous neighbours imagining shadows in the night.
No covetous men with insecure wives. She was no
witch as they defined.

They came to her forest when she was walking by
the river. Men tied her hands to her feet as she
laughed. They thought she would float. When she
started melting, the hunters howled their success.
When her roiling darkness spread across the water to
crack the earth, their howling turned to screams.

UNREQUITED SONATA

First published in *NewMyths* in September 2019

They told Deirdre she was unnatural, a freak. Her family told her she was an embarrassment. It had always been this way. Each time it whittled a tiny piece of her away and each time she wondered if there was enough left to go on.

When Deirdre got the invitation to perform solo at the Soundshell, she was sitting on the pier staring out across the bottomless lake with her long fingers tucked tight into her pockets to protect them from the chilly air. She'd been arguing with her brothers all morning. Her father had threatened to cut her inheritance if she didn't stop bringing her family into disrepute. It was bad enough that she was a female playing percussion; but to be a goblin playing *classical* music was unforgivable. The silence ricocheted off the still water, just like it had ricocheted around the room that morning.

She could hear the clockwork starling that delivered the message well before it arrived because the whirring of its wings was interrupted by a loud *thunk* every seven seconds. She watched as the glittering blue metal

bird plummeted to the side each time
the *thunk* sounded before valiantly struggling aloft
again when its wings kicked back in. There couldn't
have been a more apt analogy for her musical career.

When the defective collection of springs and cogs
finally descended towards her perch at the
pier, Deirdre had to throw her hand out to catch the
poor thing before it plummeted into the lake. The
bird's beak clattered open to deliver its message.
Deirdre gently held the bird and inspected its parts to
see if she could figure out what was wrong while she
listened to the message.

*"Dear Ms. Smigley, We are pleased to inform you that your
application for the emerging pianist scholarship to play at the
annual Soundshell Symphony has been successful. Please reply
within three days to confirm you are still available. Kind
Regards, Gregor Quarg Assistant-Director, Society for the
Performance of Sound."*

Deirdre's hands stopped moving and her gaze lifted
from the little clockwork bird back to the vista before
her. This could be it. This could be the performance
that would make all the years of concerts in school
halls and dementia homes worthwhile. This was her
chance to show her family she wasn't an
embarrassment after all.

The messenger bird started struggling in her hand,
trying to return to its sender. Deirdre extended a single
silver talon from between her fingers and pulled at a

bent spring until it looked a bit straighter. Then she let the little bird go and watched it fly away. Ten seconds later she heard a pop and watched the bird spin into a barrel roll mid-air before carrying on flying. At least it wasn't losing altitude now. She knew what it was like to keep falling just as you thought you were getting somewhere.

When her family heard the news, they told her it was political correctness gone mad; token diversity for the middle classes. A tiny voice in the back of Deirdre's mind wondered if that were true. Another whittled piece of self drifted to the floor. Their world was made up of the good and the bad and no-one crossed between. The fae might venture to the punk goblin underground for an exciting night out. The goblins might help elven hunters fend off the dragons that attacked them all. And then they all went back to where they belonged. All except for Deirdre.

Two weeks later, she stood backstage at the Soundshell waiting to perform her solo. The manager's jaw dropped when she arrived and he checked her ID three times before he let her into the building. If her kind sweated, she would have been soaking wet with nerves. Instead her hair had stiffened to form a solid halo around her head. She had anticipated that might happen and had cut it short for the occasion. Her 8-year-old cousin had mocked her as the locks fell to the bathroom floor. She had bribed him not to tell with a lizard's tail. The other peoples already thought her kind were only good for punk rock. She didn't need a nerve-ridden mohawk to reinforce the image.

She ignored the fae and elven stagehands' sideways glances as they ushered her into the wings. Before she'd had a chance to get her bearings, she was hearing the Director announce her name to the Crowd and then she was stepping out into the blinding stage lights.

The applause from the crowd petered out as she crossed the stage and they realised what she was, but she didn't notice. A rushing sound had filled her ears and all she could see was the grand piano standing before her begging to be played.

She sat down and caressed the keys for a second, careful to keep her talons sheathed. She could feel the piano's age and the dedication of the young and upcoming piano-maker that had constructed her all those years ago. How fitting that her professional debut was on a piano that had been the first of its distinguished maker's creations. She doubted any others who played her had even noticed. For all their haughty silence, the fae and elves seldom stopped to feel. Goblins felt vibrations through the earth and through time. Strummed strings and beaten drums filled the air with history that was lost on the 'good' peoples.

All she could see in the bright lights of the stage was the piano before her. She could have been alone. She placed her hands in position and began to play her composition – *Unrequited Sonata*. She had picked the piece because it was quiet, almost fragile. The opposite of what this crowd would expect from Goblin music. Distantly, she heard a small sound of surprise travel through the watching crowd.

She leaned forward into the music as she played, hammers sending shivers through the air as they hit the strings. Her fingers skipped faster and faster across the keys until the sounds from the crowd turned to gasps of delight. She felt her mind carried away on waves of rhythm as her talons started extending and retracting to play extra keys in a way she never had before. The melody split into two and then three new strands, weaving together in impossible complexity. She was a one-goblin piano orchestra.

She realised what was going on about ten seconds before the crowd. She didn't know whether to curse and rage at a world that seemed determined to crush her dreams or to revel in this moment of virtuosity that would never be repeated.

When the crowd caught on, their gasps turned to screams. They couldn't see the dragon yet, but they knew that no goblin could make music so beautiful. A tear splashed down onto the piano as Deirdre surrendered to despair. She was capable of beauty all on her own, but no-one would believe it now.

High above them, a giant iridescent serpent was circling the Soundshell with sweeping wings. Each of its eyes shot forth invisible streaks of power that fell onto the peoples gathered below. Its blue eye sent a targeted beam of inspiration down to Deirdre at the piano. Its green eye sent a broad spray of enthrallment across Deirdre and the crowd, trapping them in their seats listening. The two strands twisted together around Deirdre's body, soaking into her skin and driving her hands to play with more and more frenzy. Those who hadn't run already could no longer break free.

The dragon dove down into the crowd and picked up its first victim with a crunch of bone. Deirdre's tears came faster as she listened to the screams. Even if she survived, all that would be remembered was the goblin who thought she could play classical music and enthralled her audience to their deaths instead. Dragons were notorious gluttons and there was no telling how many people this particular dragon could consume in one meal. She couldn't even tear her eyes from the keys long enough to see how big it was.

As the music continued to tear itself out of her, she became aware of a whirring noise next to her ear that was slightly out of time. She was almost annoyed enough to raise a hand from the keys to swat the distraction away, but the dragon's power held her hands to their task. The whirring clockwork starling landed on the music stand before her. Now that it was in her field of vision, she could see its head was cocked to the side slightly. Its beak clattering in anxiety.

Deirdre couldn't stand the bird's distracting rhythms. "Go away! You're ruining the music."

The starling just clattered even louder, punctuating the sounds with confused whistles.

"The dragon is making my music enthral the crowd so it can feed," Deirdre said in answer to the wordless query.

She hoped the silly bird would leave her alone once it knew what was going on. The starling stopped clacking and whistling for a moment and turned its head to stare at Deirdre with one black eye. Then it launched itself into the air. Deirdre leaned forward again into her playing. She could feel the spaces between her fingers starting to bleed as her talons whirred in and out. She watched the red liquid drip between the keys.

If she had been able to look away from the piano, she would have stared in amazement at what happened next. The tiny clockwork starling landed on a wall near the dragon who was finishing its appetiser nearby. When the dragon launched itself back into the air, the starling followed. The dragon circled overhead, savouring the anticipation of its meal waiting below.

The mechanical starling flew the length of the Soundshell away and hovered watching the dragon. Then it launched itself like an arrow through the air. Ten seconds it flew. It was mid-barrel roll as it hit the dragon's glowing emerald green eye with its sharp steel beak. It wasn't big enough to cause any real damage, but even dragons don't like having their eyeball scratched. It blinked back tears as it veered off course and in that moment the crowd below was released from its thrall. They screamed and scattered for the safety of the nearby buildings.

Deirdre sat at the piano still playing. She was no longer enthralled, but the inspiration was still flowing from the dragon's blue eye and she couldn't tear herself away. It wasn't until the dented starling dropped onto the piano's soundboard with a crack that she finally paused and looked up. She reached out a hand to the starling and watched the blood from her fingers mix with the dragon eye-gunk that had clogged the bird's mechanics. Its whistles were reduced to gurgling static.

A shadow fell over them both and Deirdre picked up the starling and threw herself to the side just in time to avoid the dragon's snapping jaws. With her self-preservation instincts finally restored, Deirdre sprinted for the stage wings and the safety of the solid stone walls of the theatre building beyond.

Deirdre stumbled through the hallways in a haze of confusion. When she came across a restroom, she used it to clean up her hands and the little clockwork bird as best she could. The sticky liquid from the dragon's eye had started eating away at its metals, leaving them tarnished and rusting.

The Director found her there cradling the little starling in her hands. She held out a hand to the dazed goblin and pulled her up to her feet. The dragon had abandoned the Soundshell before the military forces could move in to retaliate. He was a lazy dragon, used to feasting on the catatonically enthralled. Chasing prey was not his thing. When the media managed to piece together what had happened, the headlines read *Soundshell massacre averted by Goblin's clockwork kindness.*

Deirdre read the article with a sinking heart. She was a hero, but the article didn't even mention her piano performance. The few bookings she had following the night at the Soundshell had all been cancelled, as if she might somehow attract another dragon. Her brother had called by to ask if she had finally come to her senses. It went without saying that heroic kindness hadn't really helped the embarrassment levels of her goblin family. Deirdre's head drooped forward as she contemplated her future. Maybe it was time to give up the dream.

The clockwork starling had followed her home and seemed determined to stay. It flew to her shoulder and ran its beak through her hair, pulling several strands out when they caught in its springs.

She sat down at her piano and placed her fingers gently on the keys. She hadn't played since the dragon's attack. She tried to play *Unrequited Sonata* again. The piece sounded incomplete without the complexity of the extra melodies. She slowed the piece down and extended a talon tentatively towards a key as she played, and then another. It was awkward, but if she angled her fingers just right she could play the extra notes without messing up the main melody.

Her talons could spread far wider than her normal range, creating new chords as she explored. She played a few bars and then grabbed a pencil to start scrawling notations on the sheet music in front of her. She couldn't play the way the dragon had made her play, but she could still play in a way that no-one else ever had. Sometimes when you whittle everything else away and you feel dead inside, it is because all that is left is the heartwood – enduring, resonant, and strong as steel. It is pure potential that can be anything you craft it to be.

Deirdre could feel when her piece was ready for the world, melodies and harmonies weaving together until the heartache she had captured was amplified far beyond the sum of each individual strand. When she auditioned the piece, there was no way the Director could say no to that raw emotion. No way she could deny the tears streaming down her face, or her shaking hands as she booked Deirdre in to play.

When the night of her performance arrived, Deirdre's hair lay flat and calm. She had nothing to prove to herself or anyone else anymore. From the first note, the crowd sat enthralled. There was no question that the beauty of that music was all her own. The rapt audience was silent for long seconds when she raised her hands from the keys. Their thundering applause when it came startled her clockwork bird into flight, making it fly circles around her hair that was now undulating with excitement.

The next day she hit the headlines again: *Goblin Starts Biggest Music Revolution Since Punk Rock.* Even her family could be proud of that.

GREEN IS MORE THAN SKIN DEEP

First published in *Curses & Cauldrons* from Blood
Song Books in August 2019

Agnes pulled another splinter from her thigh and
winced. Life had been easier with metal-handled
brooms and plastic bristles. The greenies had taken
over and they were all back to birch twigs and ash.
Snap a twig in strong winds and you would pitch
sideways till you spiralled in the air. She tried to take a
swig of potion from her keep cup, but nothing came
out. The tip of a lizard's tail was wedged in the no-spill
hole. She looked down at an ocean of rubbish, choking
the world. Maybe it was worth it. Time to get to work.

THE FISHER

First published in *newsroom* in October 2019
Reprinted in *Year's Best Aotearoa New Zealand Science
Fiction and Fantasy Volume 2*
Reprinted in *The Best of British Fantasy 2019*
Finalist, Best Short Story, Sir Julius Vogel Awards

It was Wednesday and a man was standing on a small
rock jutting out of the ocean a few metres from the
beach in Oriental Bay. He had a fishing rod in his
hands and an old paint bucket by his side for when his
luck found him. He was wearing a tatty blue and
purple jacket that looked like it wouldn't keep the
water out at all.

Neil disguised himself in his wife's old jacket and came
down to the beach to fish one day every second
month. His wife thought he was at work and his
workmates thought he was at home. The stresses of
both were lost in the noise of the waves crashing and
the anticipation of success. At the end of the day, he
would take his catch to a local homeless shelter,
change back into his suit and go home for dinner.

His wife was grateful that he came home early every once in a while. They were more like flatmates than husband and wife these days. She would try not to start up old arguments that day, although her mind couldn't help but save them up for the next. Maybe this was the Wednesday she would bring up having children again. Surely a child would close the gap that had grown between them.

In two months' time, his wife would go for a walk along the beach and see him standing on a rock fishing. She would feel betrayed, but at least they would have something new to talk about.

◎

Jack lost his job three months ago, right around the time his fourth child was born. He'd suffered a brain injury at work and never gone back. His jacket came from the free bin outside a thrift store and his hands ached from the cold. He walked an hour to the beach to fish every day. His wife was breastfeeding and needed the protein. He'd heard fish oil could help with depression. Sometimes he thought if he ate fish one more time he would scream.

Each night as he walked up to his front door, he wondered if his family would still be there to greet him. His wife was exhausted and kept asking him to stay home and help. She glanced sideways at Jack as they sat on the couch watching tv, but only when she thought he wouldn't notice. She wondered if he would ever be the man he used to be.

That Wednesday, she took the kids down to the beach to see him. They dug for pipis in the sand and pestered their dad to sing. She rolled her sweatpants up and waded to his rock in the ocean to take his hand.

"Come on. Let's go home," she said.

Steve's Grandmother taught him about kai moana, the foods from the sea, when he was a little boy. Her tangi was two weeks ago. He had not been home for years and he cried almost as much for the memories he had lost as for her death.

He'd called in sick from his city job to stand on that rock and fish. It was a different ocean to the one at home, but if he closed his eyes the sounds of the waves and gulls calling started to restore his memories. He hadn't worn the jacket in ten years. Even all these years later it still smelled of teenage angst. Its scent mixed with the smells of bait and seaweed to make him feel slightly ill. That brought memories back too.

His boyfriend was reading a book further up the beach, wrapped in the red picnic blanket they always carried in the boot of their car. When Steve grew tired of standing on the rock, he waded back to shore and sat with him. He told him about the fragments of his childhood on a wild coastline that had returned to him, and his boyfriend added his own. They had never realised they had this in common.

Two years later, Steve would propose at that same spot and six months after that they would exchange vows and rings with the sea breeze blowing around them. The rock sticking out of the ocean was just big enough for two men to stand with arms wrapped around each other, smiling into the wide-angle lens that would capture all 180 degrees of memory-restoring ocean.

Poseidon was far from home and searching for his lost trident. He was hoping if he stood out of the water in disguise that Tangaroa would not notice his encroachment in this ocean. Who would think a God would wear such a tatty jacket?

He had followed the trail of earthquakes up New Zealand from Christchurch, through to Hurunui and Kaikōura. Now he stood on a rock in Wellington harbour hoping he could get the trident back before the next earthquake struck. He wasn't against earthquakes generally, unless someone made them happen with his stolen property. He didn't know who had stolen the trident. It could be Tangaroa for all he knew, but he hoped it wasn't. That would be awkward.

As he stood there fishing, the rod bent and he started reeling in the line. His muscles strained and his eyes narrowed as he realised whoever was holding the trident might be as strong as he was. He'd been reeling for 10 minutes when he felt a tremor travel through the rock underneath him. He looked across the harbour just as the pier in the main business district crumbled into the ocean.

"Fuck," he said, and started reeling faster. The water around him receded out into Cook Strait, leaving him stranded on a rock surrounded by sand. He could feel the ocean preparing to lever itself up to flood the city quays lined with high-rise buildings. A tsunami-warning siren wailed in the distance.

He sighed in frustration. He may as well make the most of it though. He fashioned himself a surfboard from the sands around him, melding it into golden glass. Then he rode the 20-foot waves into the city as if it had been his idea all along.

Kate lies on a smooth hard surface. The man, the fishing rod and the bucket aren't even real. They are just a virtual construct created for a woman who yearns for the days when the oceans were full of life; days she hadn't been alive to see.

Does the jacket have special meaning to her? Perhaps it came from researching her family history. Or perhaps it was just made up by the author of the construct to give authenticity to an environment he had never experienced. Just another line of code.

The ocean and the sky start to flicker and then disappear. Kate sits up in a room with plain white walls, ceiling, and floor and pulls her headset off.

"I wasn't finished, I didn't even see a fish," she yells to the empty room. "And why the hell did you make me a man?"

Only static comes from the room's hidden speakers. The door opens to tell her it is time to leave.

"Bloody budget VR companies," she mutters as she returns to her apartment.

It won't stop her coming back month after month though, spending her savings to search a virtual construct for anything that might make her life more real.

Jeremy lies in a hospital somewhere. The scene at the beach is part of a years-long timeline that plays through his head in the hours between when he loses consciousness and when he regains it.

He stands on the rock with his son, teaching him how to fish. It was a spur of the moment trip. He'd grabbed the jacket from a bag of old clothes they had cleared from his mother's house after she died. He should have taken it to the dump months ago, but he couldn't bring himself to throw it away. They only stay ten minutes before the cold gets to be too much and he piggy-backs his son to the shore.

In a few hours, he will wake in the hospital to find he has never had any children. He will stifle his great heaving sobs in his pillow until his chest aches and he is dizzy from lack of air. One of the nurses will find him sobbing and hold him tight to her, even though she knows she shouldn't.

Their first child will be a boy. Jeremy's mother will come to stay for three weeks when he's born. She will snuggle the baby close under her jacket to protect him from the wind when they take him for his first trip to the beach.

It was Wednesday and a man was standing on a small rock jutting out of the ocean wearing a tatty blue and purple jacket that looked like it wouldn't keep the water out at all.

BIG BROTHER

First published in *National Flash Fiction Day*
MicroMadness finalists in June 2019

Margaret watched the tired woman push her baby towards playgroup. She handed Amanda a coffee as she entered "How are you?"

"Fine, Tommy is learning to stand." Amanda tugged her sleeve down over the flashing emotion-monitor on her wrist a moment too late. Margaret saw and pulled the woman into a hug "No, you're not. How long has the depression alarm been going?"

Amanda's shoulders slumped "A day maybe."

"We don't have much time then. Come on, let's talk it through."

Amanda held tight to her son and followed Margaret as her eyes looked behind her for child services.

WOULD SHE BE GONE

A Censored City Novelette

CHAPTER 1

"Are you sure you're up for this, Detective? Wires and comms won't work there. You won't be able to call for back-up if things go south."

Gini squared her shoulders and stood a little straighter. She knew the risks. This was the opportunity of a lifetime—undercover surveillance of a major crime syndicate. She might even get a medal out of it. It would make all the sacrifices worthwhile.

"Understood, Captain. You can count on me," she replied.

Captain Anders reached out to shake her hand. "We're behind you all the way, Detective. We need this win. You've got 20 minutes to prep. Detective Palmer will be your handler for the mission. Stay undercover as long as it takes. Dismissed."

Gini fought to keep her face to an appropriate expression as she left the room. She should have realised the operation was too good to be true. This was worth putting up with Palmer for, though.

Fifteen minutes later, she was pulling at the unfamiliar black wool turtleneck where it rubbed against her throat. She wondered how people wore this kind of thing every day. Her phone vibrated in her pocket and she checked the message.

Dad's not doing great. You coming tomorrow?

Her fingers stabbed at the screen as she typed a reply. The last thing she needed right now was a family drama.

I said I would. I'm working. Can't talk.

She'd barely hit send before the reply came.

You're always working. You better be there.

"Everything OK, Gin?" Palmer's voice called from behind her.

Gini spun around. "Of course, *Detective*."

"Oh. We're like that now?"

"Professional? Yeah."

Palmer shook his head. "Look, I said I'm sorry. Excuse me for thinking I had a right to care about you as a person. Is this going to be a problem?"

"No problem. Like I said—professional."

Palmer stared at her, and then sighed and looked away. "Fine. I'll take a different route to the meet and park on the corner of Jefferson and 7th. If you need me to follow you when you leave, take off your hat. Otherwise, we can debrief tomorrow in the park."

"Great," Gini said.

"It's not like I could have avoided talking to him, Gin. What was I supposed to do? Sit there in your lounge in a towel in silence?"

"Professional," Gini said again, and she turned and walked to her car.

She heard Palmer sigh again behind her, but he didn't call after her. What should he have done? Not open her damn door, especially to her brother. What gave him the right? She slammed her car door shut and pulled out of the carpark.

She was still fuming when she pulled into a park across from the bar. She sat gripping the steering wheel, breathing deeply. There was too much riding on this operation to let anything personal get in the way. She pulled on her black flat cap, used her mirror to apply a bright red lipstick and focused on who she needed to be. She steadied her hands and relaxed her face. By the time she was sauntering across the road, she doubted her squad would have recognised her.

The doorman inspected her inside the entrance to the bar.

"When to the sessions of sweet silent thought," Gini said, softly.

He looked her up and down. "All losses are restored and sorrows end. A good choice. You're new here. Who's your sponsor?"

Gini scrambled for an answer. No-one had mentioned a sponsor. She didn't even know where their intel had come from. It was that classified.

"Shakespeare," she said, raising her eyebrow as if she couldn't believe he'd asked the question.

"Sorry, I have to check. Can't be too careful. You'd be surprised how many newbies start naming people. Hand me your cell phone and you can head inside," the doorman said.

Gini passed her phone over and he placed it in a locker behind the desk.

"I just need to do a quick search before you go in," he said as he handed her a receipt for the phone.

She inspected the handheld device he was using as he meticulously scanned her. They had the latest tech. She wondered where they'd got it from. There was no way she could have snuck a recording device in.

"All clear. Enjoy your night."

She headed into the bar and ordered a glass of Pinot Noir before settling herself at a small table in a back corner away from the stage. She needed to avoid drawing attention to herself before she got the lay of the land. There were almost 50 people mingling or sitting at the other tables. She was surprised there were so many.

The polished wood of the tables gleamed in the flickering light from tealight candles and the thick red curtains by the stage looked like they would stand up to scrutiny in daylight. It wasn't exactly the dive she had pictured. The clientele was exactly as she had pictured them, though. The Gatsby hat had been the perfect choice to blend in. Hats and scarves abounded—anything they could use to hide their faces when they left.

Her glass was half empty when a man stepped up to the stage and began to speak.

"Welcome. Tonight's theme, as you know, is drawn from Shakespeare. In sonnet 66, he wrote:

And art made tongue-tied by authority,
And folly, doctor-like, controlling skill,
And simple truth miscalled simplicity,
And captive good attending captain ill:
　Tired with all these, from these would I be gone,
　Save that, to die, I leave my love alone.

I think those words speak down the ages to us here. Tonight, art will not be made tongue-tied by authority. There is no algorithm here deciding what you may hear or not. With your discretion, our poets will not be captive good. They will not be arrested for daring to speak to an audience that cares to listen. Because you do care. You care about freedom of speech and expression. You care about art and simple truth. Please, welcome our first poet!"

Gini took another sip of wine as applause sounded around her. She had to do something to cover her eye-roll response to that speech. Typical anarchists relying on the old 'freedom of speech' adage as if anyone was controlling what drivel these poets and authors produced. Just because they had a right to speak, didn't mean they had a right to inflict their words on the vulnerable. All the Librarian algorithm did was protect the vulnerable from mental health triggers—be they triggers of trauma or crime. It saved lives, unlike these so-called poets.

Gini got her anger back under control and paid attention to the stage again. A woman in her sixties was standing in front of the microphone adjusting the stand height. Her long grey hair was loose, partially screening her face from the watching crowd. She stood for a moment, composing herself, and then started to speak.

"I crashed a car at eighteen.

Quick, hide that Harry Potter and the willow scene,

and any other book where trauma is foreseen;

a literary vaccine.

Which is great, if the Librarian is free

from all subjective judgements and can see,

with unerring clarity,

every way in which those words I read have meaning to me.

Does your algorithm see inside my head?

Was it there the day I read my father Vonnegut on his deathbed?

Because the books you let him access could not distract him from his dread.

No. Instead,

You tore me from his dying exhalation.

Charged me with solicitation.

Ignored the comfort given by my narration.

And, in final insult, denied my right to be present at his cremation."

The woman's voice was cracking with emotion, the last word but a sobbed whisper. Gini reached up to scratch her cheek and frowned in surprise to find it wet. She swiped at the tear. It was just because the anniversary was so close, she thought. She didn't have anything in common with this woman. She had missed her mother's funeral for an entirely different reason. A valid reason. Unlike this lawbreaker.

A man who'd been leaning on the wall nearby approached her. "It can be pretty intense your first time," he said softly, offering her a tissue.

Gini forced herself to focus back on her mission and looked up at him, letting another tear leak out.

"Yeah. I hadn't really thought I'd be affected like that."

The first poet had left the stage and their place had been taken by the next.

"My name's Jonas. Mind if I join you?" the man asked.

"I'd like that. I'm Katherine. My friends call me Kat," Gini said with a smile.

She watched him surreptitiously as the next poet spoke. He had a hipster beard and a ridiculous flop of hair hanging down his forehead. Didn't these people even try to hide what they were? When the poet finished his performance, Jonas clicked his fingers in appreciation. Gini covered another eye-roll with her wine glass.

"I love the way his performance makes you forget the microphone is even there. He uses such mundane words, but it feels so intimate," Jonas said.

Gini had prepared for a conversation like this, drawing on distant memories of her mother from when she was a teenager.

"The language is what makes it intimate. As if he's talking to someone he's lived with forever. The rhythm is what keeps you hanging though."

"It reminds me a little of some of the rhythms Woolf used in her works. Do you think so?"

"I can't access them," Gini said with an ironic grin.

"Seriously? That's ridiculous!"

The people at the table next to them glared at Jonas for the loud outburst. The next poet was about to start.

"My mother was a writer who killed herself," Gini muttered with an awkward shrug.

The Captain had insisted she use her real history to ingratiate herself with these people. He'd said it would seem more authentic. Gini had almost told him to stuff his mission.

"I'm so sorry. I see why you reacted to Lauren's poem now," Jonas whispered back.

His face was set in that expression Gini hated. The one her workmates had worn for days after she missed the funeral, as if they could understand her loss. Damn the captain for being right.

"I lost my mother when I was 12. I don't think you ever really get over it," Jonas said.

Gini's eyes widened and Jonas gave her a sad smile of shared pain before returning his gaze to the stage. She let the emotions of the poet's words act as white noise for her own and ignored the niggle of guilt Jonas's words had set off inside her. It didn't matter that they had something in common. He was breaking the law just as much as anyone else here.

The MC came out to give a final speech at the end of the performance. Gini barely heard him as she tried to decide what the right play was with Jonas. If she came on too strong, she might give herself away. When the applause faded, the audience stood and reached for their jackets.

"See you next time?" Jonas asked.

"For sure."

He tilted his head to the side and inspected her as if he was weighing how dangerous she might be. Then he reached in his pocket and grabbed a card.

"This is my number if you ever want to talk. I could get my hands on some Woolf for you, too. Or whatever else you were interested in."

Their fingers brushed as Gini took the card and she smiled. She couldn't believe it had been that easy. This could bust their case wide open.

"Thanks, Jonas. It was lovely to meet you," she said

Jonas leaned forward and kissed her on the cheek before waving goodbye.

She kept her hat on as she left the bar. Once she was safely in her car, she reached up to take it off. She was so lost in thought that she didn't notice her fingers lingering on the spot Jonas had kissed.

CHAPTER 2

The next day, Gini paused in her morning jog through the park to stretch under the shade of an oak tree. Palmer appeared a few minutes later.

"What took you so long? No-one stretches for this long mid-jog," Gini hissed at him.

"How'd it go? Got any leads?"

"I met a guy," Gini said.

"An important guy?"

Gini smirked at the hint of jealousy in his voice. This was going to be more fun than she'd thought.

"I don't know, yet. I've got to take it slow. I don't want to arouse suspicion."

"Shouldn't be a problem for you. Taking it slow has always been your strong suit."

Gini glared at him and turned her back to jog off.

"Wait! I'm sorry. That was unprofessional," Palmer said.

Gini paused and looked back at him. "Yes. It was."

"Do you need a ride to your dad's? You could have a few drinks with them. Relax a bit."

"For the last time. My family is none of your business. Back off!"

This time she didn't turn around when he called out after her.

She almost wished she'd taken him up on his offer when she arrived at her dad's that afternoon. He was sitting on the couch with her brother looking at pictures of her mum. Two empty bottles of wine nearby suggested they'd been there a while. They both looked up as she walked in and she felt the same old stab of grief and anger. Why did they have to wallow in memories of her? It was like picking at an infected scab.

"Hi, sweetheart," her dad said.

"You made it," her brother added.

"I said I would, didn't I?"

The two men on the couch exchanged a look and then returned to looking at the album.

"I can't stay long. Work's really busy," Gini said.

"Of course, it is," her brother said, his face twisting with sarcasm.

"That's enough, George," her dad said. He carefully enunciated each syllable, but Gini could still hear the drunken slur.

"So, what's the deal? What kind of memorial are we doing?" Gini asked.

"Always in a hurry to get away," George sniped.

"I said enough!"

Gini looked at her father in surprise. It wasn't like him to get angry. She could see the tension in his face, as if he was bracing himself.

"Dad. You're upset. We don't have to do this today."

George snorted back sarcastic laughter and their dad glared at him again.

"It's the anniversary. We're doing it today. Sit down!"

Gini sighed and sunk into a nearby armchair. It was the one her mother used to curl up in and write. Everything here was tainted with memories of her.

"You've avoided this long enough. We are remembering her properly today. Like we should have at the funeral."

Gini burned with shame. Her fingers picked at a loose thread in the armrest.

"I couldn't be there, Dad. I had to work. I didn't have any choice."

"You have a choice now. You don't even have to do anything. Just close your eyes and listen. Like she used to."

Gini winced. There was no getting out of this. She shouldn't have driven there. She could have been drunk. She'd done this to herself.

When she was a girl, she used to try and write stories and poems like her mother. Her mum had always said stories were made to be spoken. She would listen in careful silence with her eyes closed as Gini recited her latest attempt. Gini would hold her breath after she finished reciting and watch for the moment her mother's eyes would open and a brilliant smile would flash across her face.

"I don't need to close my eyes," she said through the aching pain in her throat.

"Please," her father added.

She sighed. "Fine."

She leaned back in the chair and shut her eyes. She heard her dad rustling in a bag nearby and then silence descended. Her breathing deepened as the quiet stretched to wrap around them like the blanket she used to nestle under when her mother read to her. Gini started as her father's soft voice sounded from nearby.

"There is a hole inside me, somewhere. A singularity that draws in all it touches. And everything that is me hovers on its edge, just past its event horizon—containing it even as it consumes me. I watch the light trickle out of the world like the vestiges of a draining ocean, leaving only memories flopping on the sand like drowning fish."

Gini was held captive by the voice and the words. She'd never heard her father speak like this before. As if he understood exactly how she felt every day, and felt that way himself too.

"And in the distance, I see figures moving. They carry buckets of water to pour upon the gasping fish, even though each bucket barely lasts a breath before it sinks into the grains of sand. I love those figures more than anything. I love each precious memory they protect. For a time, their love anchors me against the horizon's lure."

Gini felt her stomach drop down through the floor. This didn't sound like her dad. Her eyes flew open and she stared at him on the couch, holding a reader in his hands. A reader that wasn't his. For a moment, her professional-self wondered where he'd found a black-market reader and if Jonas was involved. Then panic set in. She was frozen in place.

"No, no, no. What have you done, Dad? Stop!" By the time she reached the last word, she was screaming.

He looked up from the reader. "You have a right to hear your mother's words, Virginia. No government should take that away from you. We got this reader for you. So you can make peace with her."

"I've got my work phone in my pocket, Dad! It monitors everything. The Librarian will have triggered an alarm already."

"But you wouldn't have listened if you knew what I was reading," her Dad replied, as if that explained anything.

"You would have kept pretending she was trying to hurt us. That she didn't care at all," George muttered.

She could see the heartbreak in his face. Gini opened her mouth to reply, but she was interrupted by the front door crashing open. She instinctively reached for the gun she wasn't wearing before she realised the people bursting into the room were police officers and raised her hands in the air.

"Edward Wright. You are under arrest for possession of an illegal reader and literary solicitation. You have the right to remain silent…"

Gini stared in shock as her frail father's wrists were twisted behind his back and handcuffed. The voice was relentless.

"George Wright. You are under arrest for aiding and abetting in literary solicitation…"

"No," Gini whispered. She closed her eyes and slumped back into her chair as the arrest carried on relentlessly.

"Detective Wright?" the voice asked, finally.

She looked up. She recognised the officer from her tour of cyber-crimes when she was first offered the undercover position.

"Jennings," she said in greeting.

"You're suspended until we can review all evidence and confirm you weren't involved. Hand over your badge and gun."

Gini stood up and pushed past him. "I'm on an undercover op. They're at the precinct already."

By the time she got outside, the patrol cars were already pulling away with the last of her family inside. She stood on the sidewalk staring after them. She was still standing there when Detective Jennings emerged from the house.

"What was he reading you anyway?"

"None of your damn business."

"Suit yourself. I'll hear when you give evidence at the trial anyway. The Captain said to tell you to book in for a psych eval while you're waiting to be cleared."

Gini peered closer at Jenning's expression. Her brain was slowly kicking back into gear.

"How did you get here so fast? And why aren't you arresting me? That's not protocol."

"Don't overthink it, Wright."

"Holy shit. This was a sting operation, wasn't it? Were my family the target or just collateral? Was anyone going to tell me?" Gini said.

"Go home, Wright. We'll call you when you're cleared."

Palmer was waiting by the door of her apartment when she got there.

"Did you know?" she asked.

"I knew there was another undercover operation going down. I didn't know they were arresting your family until they called me an hour ago. I swear."

Gini's hands were shaking so hard she fumbled the key in the lock. Palmer reached out to help.

"Back off! What are you even doing here? I'm suspended. Go *handle* someone else."

"Come on, Gin. Let me in. That's what friends do."

"I told you we're done."

"Yeah, well. You don't get to decide when I stop caring."

Gini glared at him, but Palmer already had his foot against the door to stop it closing. She threw the door open so hard it crashed into the wall and stalked to the kitchen to find the whiskey. Palmer was leaning on the doorframe watching her when she turned around with a full glass.

"You know, if you talk to me I can tell the Captain you don't need the psych eval," he said.

Gini swore under her breath. "Fine."

She shoved an empty glass at him and went back to the lounge. Palmer joined her on the couch a moment later and Gini shifted sideways until she was wedged into the corner.

"So, what did they get them for?" he asked.

"Possession and solicitation."

Palmer winced. "Damn. That's not good. Can't argue it's not premeditated with possession."

"Thanks. That's really reassuring. I feel so much better now. Are we done yet?" Gini slammed back the rest of her whiskey in one go.

"No. We're not done. What were they reading you?"

Gini stared at the dregs of amber liquid in her glass. She didn't want to talk to Palmer about it. She didn't want to talk to anyone about it. A psych eval would be worse though. Last time she'd barely scraped through.

"Something my mother wrote," she said.

"Oh, Gin. I'm sorry."

Gini got up to fetch the bottle of whiskey from the kitchen and poured herself another glass. She wished the lounge had enough room for more than a single sofa. When she got back, she avoided the couch and sat on the floor leaning against the wall. The last thing she needed was Palmer trying to hug her.

"Was it about... what she did?"

"Yeah. I think so. He didn't get all the way through it."

"Do you want to read the rest of it?"

"I can't," Gini snapped.

"That's not what I asked."

Gini took another sip of her drink. At least he wasn't hiding what we wanted to know. What the Captain needed to know. She would have seen through it if he had anyway.

"No. I don't want to read the rest of it. The whole point of the Librarian is to spare me that pain. What she wrote... it's exactly how I feel when I think about her. I don't want to read how that feeling turns into what she did. It could only end badly. I don't want to think about her at all. I just want to work."

Gini slammed back another whiskey and looked over at Palmer. His face looked pained. She poured herself another drink.

"What? No come back? No intrusive questions?" she asked when the silence had stretched too long.

"Gin, I think you need to talk to someone professional. Work can't be the thing that keeps you together. You can't just ignore that pain forever."

"Yes, I can. That's what the Librarian lets me do. That's why it's there."

"The Librarian is there to make space while you heal. That's not what you're doing." Palmer said.

"Really? Because my brother talked to people. He healed. And they still arrested him."

"Your brother had read it already. He told me about it when you were in the shower. We agreed it would be good for you to read when you were ready. He was trying to help you. He just went about it the wrong way."

The sounds of traffic in the background faded as a rushing filled Gini's ears. She dropped the heavy glass from numb fingers and watched as drops of liquid sprayed across the rug. The red wool made the amber whiskey look like old blood.

"Get out," she whispered.

"Gin, stop it. Stop pushing me away. I'm all you've got right now."

Gini launched herself to her feet and stood with shaking fists by her sides. What gave him the right to discuss her pain with her brother?

"You are going to leave. You are going to tell the Captain I am fit for work. Or I will tell him you encouraged my brother to commit a crime. You might not be fired, but there's no way they'll keep you on the taskforce if there's even a chance it's true. Get out. Now." Her voice was flat and her eyes were dead as she stared down at him.

Palmer's mouth dropped open. "You can't be serious. I didn't encourage him to do anything. I told him to share it when the Librarian gave you both access. When you'd healed. Calm down!"

Gini picked up her phone and started dialling.

"Stop! Fine. Have it your way. But I'm done trying to help you."

"I never wanted your help in the first place. The door's that way." Her hands weren't shaking anymore as she pointed. She was back in control.

Palmer shook his head and pushed past her outstretched arm as he left. "Goodbye, Detective."

"See you at work, Palmer."

CHAPTER 3

Whatever Palmer said to the Captain worked because she was reinstated two days later. She was sleeping on the couch when the call came. She knocked over an empty bottle of whiskey as she tried to grab for the phone and clutch her aching head at the same time.

"Detective Wright, you are cleared to continue your operation. Re-establish contact and proceed as planned," Palmer said.

"Copy that," Gini said and winced at the huskiness that came out in her voice.

"Are you drunk, Detective?" Palmer asked.

"Goodbye, Palmer."

Gini staggered to the bathroom and turned the shower on as hard as it would go. The needling points of water on her face drove her brain fog away. She checked the clock when she got out. Almost lunchtime. There was plenty of time to sober up before she reached out to Jonas tonight.

She went for a long run to clear her head and then fetched her new burner cell from the drawer she'd thrown it in the day before. She didn't trust Palmer anymore and she wasn't going to set up a meet on a phone he was monitoring. As far as he was concerned, she was taking it slow and she wouldn't have anything to report until the next poetry slam on Saturday.

Hi, Jonas. It's Kat. I've been thinking about your offer. I'd like to take you up on it, she texted.

She couldn't say anything more direct. A real buyer wouldn't risk the message being intercepted. She didn't have long to wait for an answer.

Sure. I'll be at the Vagabond tonight. Fancy a drink?

Gini frowned. She wasn't sure if they were just organising a clandestine meeting or if he was actually asking her out. It probably didn't matter one way or the other. She needed him to trust her. As far as she knew, the Vagabond was a legal music venue. There shouldn't be any risk of being caught in another sting.

See you at ten.

She abandoned sobering up around eight and had another couple of drinks before donning Kat's irritating tight clothes, hat and bright lipstick. She glanced at her police issued phone sitting on the table on her way out the door and left it where it was. She paused in the hallway. She wouldn't put it past Palmer to be surveilling her apartment to "keep her safe".

She headed up the stairs to the roof and made her way across two adjacent buildings and down a fire escape out of sight of any of the exits from her apartment. She had picked her home carefully. Palmer thought it was for the fire escape attached to her lounge window and the basement car park exit onto a back alley. She wondered which one he was watching. Probably the alley. That's the way she'd left after their first big argument. She always made sure her house-guests thought they knew her 'secret' ways out. There were six different buildings she could exit from along the rooftops. Seven if she didn't mind risking a one-story jump.

She was fashionably late to the meet, but Jonas didn't seem to mind. He was standing at a bar leaner with a couple of other men. They had obviously been drinking for a while because he threw his arms wide when he saw her and pulled her in to kiss both cheeks like they were in Europe or something. Gini was glad she'd had a couple herself already or she might have hit him. That's what she told herself anyway. Just like she told herself the smile breaking across her face when she saw him was just acting for the operation.

"Kat! You made it! What can I get you?"

She glanced at the table and saw three whiskey tumblers. "I'd love a whiskey. What are you drinking?"

"I like her already! It's a 20-year single malt from a small distillery a couple of hours away. They grow their own barley. I'm Pete by the way," the man to Jonas's left said, reaching out to shake her hand.

"And I'm Carlos. Don't listen to Pete. He wouldn't know his bourbon from his sherry casks," the other man said.

Pete punched Carlos' arm. Jonas laughed and steered her towards the bar and away from the sounds of his friend's bickering.

"Sorry about that. If you get them started on whiskey talk, it's all downhill from there," Jonas said.

His hand was resting lightly on the small of her back as they navigated the crowd and Gini smiled back at his too close face.

"No need to apologise. I'm usually more of a solitary drinker. It's nice to talk whiskey with someone," she said.

"Does that mean we have to go back and join them, or can I keep you all to myself?" Jonas leaned in close to speak softly in her ear. His words just audible past the sounds of the jazz band that had started playing on the stage.

Gini felt his warm breath on her face before he pulled back a little to watch her. His head was tilted to the side in question, and he didn't push any further as he waited for her response. Palmer's past insult sounded in Gini's head—taking it slow had always been her strong suit. Her eyes ran down the outline of Jonas's bicep through his shirt. Not just a poetry geek then. He clearly worked out. Gini laughed and wrapped an arm around him, pulling him closer and putting her other hand on his chest.

"You can keep all of me to yourself," she said.

The more they drank and danced, the more Gini felt her real personality melding into Kat's false one until she wasn't sure where one started and the other stopped. The only difference between them really was that Kat liked poetry and talked about her feelings.

Jonas already knew about her mother's death and it wasn't long before he'd extracted from her that the anniversary was only two days ago. In the darkness of a booth at the edge of the bar, she even let herself cry again in front of him, and was shocked to see his face traced with tears as well for their shared loss. No-one had ever cried with her before. She'd made sure they didn't get the chance.

Jonas shared memories of his childhood with his mother and her death—she'd found a lump one day and died three months later. He'd refused to go to the funeral, too angry at the world, and he'd always regretted it. They sat in silence for a minute when he finished talking, listening to the frenetic drum solo playing in the background.

"I told my family I had to work, but really I made sure I couldn't be there for her funeral. They've never forgiven me," Gini said. She'd never admitted that to anyone.

Jonas leaned in and gently kissed a salty tear on her cheek. She turned her face towards him without thinking and their lips met. His hand reached up to pull her in. Gini pushed away the cop-voice in her head telling her this was going to be trouble and the even louder voice telling her not to let anyone close. At that moment, she wasn't Gini. She wasn't anyone. She had no ID, no traceable phone. No-one knew where she was and she had no friends or family around to care anymore. She pushed her lips hard against his, relishing the pain of the pressure. She heard him groan in response.

"My place is three blocks away," his voice turned the statement into a question.

"What are we waiting for, then?" Gini replied. She felt his smile against her skin.

She woke the next morning on full alert before her memory caught up and she realised why she was sleeping in a strange bed. The smell of bacon drifted through the open door and she sat up, keeping the sheet pulled up to cover her chest.

She found her clothes crumpled on the floor and scooped them up so she could duck into the ensuite and get dressed. She stared at herself in the mirror— smudged lipstick and darkened eyes—and found a flannel to scrub at her face. How did people wear make-up all the time?

Jonas was putting plates on a small dining table when she left the bedroom. His hair was still damp from showering. Gini wondered how she'd slept through that. He looked up and smiled as he caught her movement.

"Morning. Come eat. If your head feels anything like mine, it will help," he said.

He leaned forward to kiss her as she joined him at the table. Gini hesitated a moment and then let him. In the sober light of morning, she was starting to realise this hadn't been her best idea. But the kiss brought back memories of the night before and she responded despite herself. Her hand knocked a fork to the ground as she reached for him, breaking the moment.

"Eggs are better hot," Jonas said, reluctantly.

"I've got plenty of time," Gini said.

She mentally kicked herself as the words came out and she felt herself smiling at him again. Maybe Palmer had been right and she did need professional help. Why couldn't she push this guy away?

Later that morning, they lay in bed together; Gini's head resting on Jonas's chest as he stroked her hair.

"I don't usually do this, you know," he said.

She looked up at him, a little surprised. She'd assumed one-night-stands were a poetry scene thing, a criminal thing.

"Me neither," she said.

"I could tell. I can see the effort it takes you to reach out," he said, softening the words with a smile in case she took it the wrong way.

Gini threw her pillow at his face. "Screw you."

She sat up, ready for the raging argument that her relationships always ended with. Instead, he just looked at her with that endlessly patient head-tilt. The one that didn't ask anything of her that she wasn't willing to give. Her scowl cracked into a rueful smile.

"Sorry. You're right, I guess."

He smiled and pulled her closer again, resting his chin on top of her head. "I'm away for work for the next couple of days, but I'd like to see you again. Are you going to the slam on Saturday?"

Gini made herself breathe calmly so she didn't give away her panic. Not a one-night-stand then. What was she getting herself into?

"Yeah. I'd like that."

Her mind was already whirling trying to figure out how to keep whatever their relationship was a secret from Palmer, who would be watching the entrance to the bar as her back-up. Jonas kissed her hair and then disentangled himself to get out of bed. She caught herself watching his naked form and looked away.

"I've got a reader here that you can have. You can access Woolf and whatever else you fancy on it. You can tell me what you think on Saturday," he said, as he detached a wall panel at the back of the closet to reach into a hidden compartment.

"Oh, wow. Are you sure?" Gini said, surprised at her sudden reluctance.

"Of course."

"This must have cost a fortune. Can I pay you something for it?"

Jonas laughed. "Don't worry about it. I get a bulk discount."

"Thank you," Gini said softly, clutching the reader to her chest with shaking hands.

Jonas sat next to her on the bed. "You look scared. Are you OK? You're way less likely to get caught reading this than turning up to a poetry slam. But if you're not comfortable, you don't have to take it."

Gini bit back a response about the exponential difference in prison time between attending a poetry session once compared to possession of an illegal reader. She scrambled for something to say that wasn't—I don't want to send you to jail for this though, you idiot.

"It's not that. It's just… I told you my mother was a writer, didn't I? I've never been able to read anything she's written. It's a little scary to hold her words in my hands."

Jonas pulled her into an embrace and held her tight. "You don't have to read anything you're not ready for. The decision is yours and no one else's."

Telling him about her mother's stories was only supposed to be a distraction, but it made her think. He was right. The decision was hers now.

"If you need anything, I'm here for you. Call me any time, OK?"

Gini shrugged and brushed away yet another tear in annoyance. When had she grown so soft?

"Promise me, Kat," he said.

"I promise," she whispered.

"Good. Now come have a shower."

Jonas made them sandwiches with the leftover bacon for lunch. When she finally opened the door to leave the apartment, he pulled her back to kiss her one more time.

"See you Saturday," he said.

His voice was firm, as if he knew she might try and back out once she left. She smiled and kissed him on the cheek, but as he closed the door behind her she spun and held it open.

"Jonas?"

"Yes."

"My real name is Gini. Virginia," she said.

His eyebrow raised a little and then he nodded.

"Nice to meet you, Gini. Most people give a false name at a slam," he said with a smile.

"Is Jonas your real name?" she asked.

"Yes."

"Would you tell me if it wasn't?" she asked.

He laughed. "Yes, Gini. I would. I was serious when I said you should call me if you need anything. You can trust me. You are now making me late for work though."

Gini smiled and kissed him through the gap in the door before making her way down the stairs and out into the daylight. It wasn't until she was two blocks away that she remembered how careless she was being. How had things gotten out of hand so quickly?

The smile drained off her face and she forced herself to refocus. She adjusted her route to take a more convoluted path back home and entered from a different building to the one she'd left from. She felt the corner of the illegal reader pushing against her side the whole way back.

CHAPTER 4

Gini's apartment felt cold and silent after the previous night. She sat on her small couch and stared at the reader in her hands. She needed to make a decision about Jonas, and she didn't think she could make it without reading the words he had returned to her through his gift of the reader. Plus, she needed to check that it did what he said it would. She'd be irresponsible not to, surely. Her father had already read plenty of the story aloud to her. Her restriction on reading her mother's works was really just a formality now anyway.

She powered up the screen and searched for Wright and the sentences she remembered from her father's reading. It was an excerpt from one of her mother's novels. The thoughts of a thinly-veiled self-modelled character.

There is a hole inside me, somewhere. A singularity that draws in all it touches… And in the distance, I see figures moving. They carry buckets of water to pour upon the gasping fish, even though each bucket barely lasts a breath before it sinks into the grains of sand. I love those figures more than anything. I love each precious memory they protect. For a time, their love anchors me against the horizon's lure.

Gini paused in her reading, waiting for the door to crash in again like last time. The silence still hung as heavy as ever. No-one was going to interrupt this time. She took a breath and continued reading.

There may come a day when I must set those figures free. Not because their arms and anchors are not strong enough, but because I cannot tolerate my black hole keeping them enslaved. Every moment spent trying to save what is already dead and worthless, instead of living in their own right.

She almost threw the screen across the room in rage. In her darkest hours, she had wondered if her mother didn't love her. If she had hated them all so much that she had taken her own life. This was so much worse. Her mother had thought she was saving her. That Gini's love and care for her was slavery. She had no right to make that choice. The chains of grief and guilt since her death were so much worse than the chains of love had ever been.

Gini sat and read. She read everything her mother had ever published. Three novels, two collections of short stories, and a book of poetry. As sleep deprivation took hold, she started arguing with the text; muttering to herself.

"No, you're wrong. Can't you see? Just give us another chance. Give me another chance. I can help you. You don't have to do it alone."

She reached the last stanza of the last poem. The last new words she would ever hear from her mother, delayed through years of censorship. She stared into the darkness, nauseous with hunger, eyes stinging with fatigue. There was nothing she could do. She had failed. Her mother was gone. Her knees curled up into her chest and her tears washed her into unconsciousness.

When she woke, her throbbing head was far worse than any hangover she'd ever had. She woke to the same thought she'd gone to sleep with: *you didn't have to do it alone.* She was damned if she was going to make the same mistakes her mother had. It was too late to help her mother, but it wasn't too late to help herself.

Her mother was right about one thing; she didn't have to spend the rest of her life enslaved. Jonas had given her something truly precious. She spent the next few days doing nothing but reading and rereading her mother's words until her phone ringing on Saturday afternoon yanked her back to reality.

"Detective? All set for another visit to the poetry underworld?" Palmer said when she answered.

"Of course."

"I'll be a block north of the bar. Same signal as last time if you need help."

"I don't need any help."

"You never think you do, Gin. Don't make me rebook that psych eval."

"Whatever."

She checked her burner phone and saw she'd missed five messages from Jonas. The final one read: *Gini? I'm worried about you. Please reply.*

I'm sorry. I disconnected while I was reading. I'll see you tonight.

Her phone buzzed barely a minute later.

Don't scare me like that! See you soon. I miss you.

She moved through her apartment like she was still asleep, staring into space as she showered and ate. She sat for five minutes on the edge of the bed with her right sock half on her foot, before shaking her head and yanking the fabric so hard it ripped a toenail. She cursed and went to the kitchen to pour herself a whiskey. She needed to get her head back in the game or Palmer was going to realise something was wrong.

When it was time to leave, she resisted the urge to take a back exit and public transport. Palmer would be watching from somewhere nearby for sure. Instead, she got into her police-issued unmarked vehicle and headed out to the bar.

Jonas was already sitting at a table when she arrived; waiting with two glasses of whiskey. There were no friends with him this time. He stood and kissed her cheek when she approached. Gini was too busy scanning the room to notice him pull away a little too quickly. Many of the crowd were the same as last time, but there were a few new faces. She had no way of knowing whether the Captain had sent another undercover officer in, or not.

She'd decided on the way there—whatever happened, she needed to make sure Palmer and the force didn't find out about Jonas. She needed to keep him safe. She owed him that much. She could figure the rest out later.

"How did your reading go?" Jonas asked.

Gini turned back to face him and took a sip of her drink to stall. Could she really trust him? She didn't have anyone else now and she was out of options.

"Life-changing," she said.

The simple word brought back all the emotions she was pushing down. Her face froze as she fought to keep control. Jonas reached out to squeeze her hand under the table.

"I hope in a good way," he said.

The first poet was about to start and Gini took the excuse to shift her chair around closer to Jonas to face the stage. She leaned close to his ear to whisper to him, letting her hair cover her face to mask the words from anyone nearby. She couldn't afford to waste any time. If Palmer or another undercover officer raised concerns, the Captain wouldn't hesitate to order a bust on the bar so the whole operation wasn't a failure.

"We need to talk. What you gave me changed everything. You changed everything. We can't be seen leaving here together."

When she looked over to gauge his response, she was surprised to see relief on his face. His broad smile, which she hadn't noticed was missing, had returned.

"How long have you known?" she said, as realisation dawned.

Her words were covered by the applause of the audience as the first poet finished. Jonas leaned towards her and gestured towards the stage as if he were commenting on the performance; his lips so close they brushed her ear.

"We suspected when you first showed up. The reader I gave you recorded your communications to Detective Palmer."

Gini glared at him. "How dare you spy on me!" she hissed.

"Is it so different from what you were going to do to me?" His voice was calm and reasonable.

"You used my mother's death to trap me."

"And you used your mother's death to lure me in when we first met."

"Is your mother even dead?" Gini said, struggling to keep her voice low. The people at the nearby tables were starting to look over at them, frowning.

"Yes," Jonas said. His voice was clipped, now, and his face had lost all expression. They sat staring at each other. No part of them touching anymore.

"I can't do this," Gini said.

She shoved her chair back and strode out of the bar; desperately hoping he remembered not to follow, even while a tiny voice inside her wished he would because it would mean he cared. She was a block away when Palmer's text came.

What happened? Why did you pull out? Is your cover compromised?

Shit, Gini thought. She needed to put him off. He couldn't find out. She needed time to figure out what she was going to do. She gritted her teeth and played to his protective bull-shit.

Someone started reading my mother's poetry aloud. Don't tell the Captain, please. It won't affect the operation. People cry in there all the time. They'll trust me more for it, Gini texted.

Are you OK? Do you want to talk about it? Palmer replied.

I'm fine. Are you going to tell the Captain?

I'll tell him it was part of a strategy. Playing the long game.

She paused with the key in the ignition as she typed a response. Then she rolled her eyes and bit the bullet. She needed him close or he would ruin everything. He needed to think they were friends.

Thanks, Cam.

I'm sorry about the other night, Gin. I've always got your back.

Gini didn't reply. She was damned if she was going to apologise to him. Thanking him was too much already.

Her burner phone buzzed with a message from Jonas on the way home. She didn't read it until she had a glass of whiskey in hand on the couch.

I'm sorry I hurt you. I'm not sorry I recorded you. You of all people should understand. I want to see you again. Ball's in your court.

Gini sat staring at the screen. She did understand. Damn him. It didn't make her any less angry. But she couldn't bear it if he left town thinking she was going to rat him out.

I get it. Your balls are safe with me.

Her mouth twitched when he replied with a laughing emoji and two kisses. Her fingers hovered over the screen.

I'm sorry, too, she wrote.

CHAPTER 5

Gini put up with Palmer's concerned texts for the rest of the weekend, ignoring them all. When her phone woke her up on Monday morning, she almost threw it across the room.

"What do you want, Palmer?" she said.

"Have you heard? I only just found out. I would have told you earlier if I knew. I promise," he said.

"What the hell are you talking about?" Gini said.

She was already pulling on her pants as she held the phone with her shoulder. She could hear in Palmer's breathless too-fast voice that something was seriously wrong.

"Your dad and your brother. They've signed a plea bargain with the DA. Sentencing is in an hour."

"But, their lawyer said they might get off with no conviction! Why the hell are they taking a plea bargain? I need to talk to them. Now!"

"It's too late, Gin. Their lawyer wasn't there when they signed. I'll meet you at the court."

Gini almost threw up from the anxiety spike when she saw the crowd gathered on the courtroom steps. It was a media circus. She'd never seen anything like it.

There was no way this was going to end well for her family.

Palmer grabbed her shoulder from behind as she walked towards the building. She almost knocked him out.

"Calm down! It's just me. Wait up," he said.

Gini spun back towards the courthouse and kept walking.

"This isn't right. What's going on?" she demanded, gesturing to the cameras.

Palmer murmured to her so the journalists wouldn't hear. "I don't know. I swear. I have no idea what's going on."

Gini took the steps two at a time and paused to listen to a reporter speaking down the lens of a camera.

"The perpetrators of the widest literary solicitation ring ever prosecuted will be sentenced in court today. Fifteen offenders are expected to plead guilty to hundreds of offences between them. The case will be the first test of the sweeping legislative reforms to the Literary Safety Act passed on Friday after a surprise last-minute amendment was pushed through to make the new laws apply retrospectively to any outstanding prosecutions. In addition to harsher penalties, the changes will see new rights for police to access the biometric data recorded by readers. Critics are calling the law a breach of universal human rights. In a statement, the Minister for Literary Safety said the changes will save lives."

The reporter finished speaking and turned away from the camera. Gini tried to carry on into the building, but the woman had already seen the moment of unguarded despair on her face as she realised her family were stuck in the middle of a political shit-storm. She stepped in front of her, blocking her way.

"Are you related to the offenders? Do you have any comment?"

Palmer stepped in front of the camera that had swung towards them, pushing Gini into the building and covering her face with his jacket.

"We'll both be fired if your cover gets blown for coming here," he hissed in her ear.

Courthouse security stopped the cameras from following them, but the reporter ran to catch up. The woman pushed her card into Gini's hand, and then stumbled back with hands raised as Palmer shoved her away.

"I'm Deanna Myers. Here's my number in case you change your mind. Call me anytime," she said. She was watching Gini's face closely, looking for any sign she might have something to say.

"Back off!" Palmer said.

"Easy, mate. Let the lady decide for herself."

Gini tucked the card into her pocket as she watched the woman walk away. Palmer put an arm around her and steered her towards the courtroom.

"I'm sure it will be OK. They weren't part of the criminal ring. They were just small-fry customers," he said.

Gini pulled away from him. "It doesn't matter what they did. It only matters what the DA put down on the form and how much the judge wants to play with their new powers. I bet they didn't even know the law had changed before they signed."

They sat in the front row of the court. Gini's body hunched inwards, expecting the blow to come. Her spine pushed back hard against the wood of the benches as she braced herself against it. The point of pain was a lifeline of feeling as her mind went numb.

She didn't even notice the tears running freely down her cheeks when her father and brother entered the docks. They saw her there and tried to smile, but they must have realised something wasn't right. The flashes from court photographers filled the air like lightning as the pressure built. Palmer whispered to remind her to keep her face turned away from the cameras. He had to pull her to her feet when the judge entered.

The ritual of the court passed in a blur that Gini struggled to follow. She didn't wake from her daze until the collective gasp from the crowd behind her made her start. The first offender had been sentenced—25 years. Five times longer than any previous sentence, likely five times longer than the man had agreed with the DA. The judge was sending a message.

"He was the head of the operation. He won't do that to your family. It will be OK," Palmer whispered. He didn't sound like he believed it, though.

Her father and brother were the last to be sentenced. Her father was swaying as he stood, in shock from what had just occurred.

"Edward Wright, you plead guilty to one count each of solicitation and possession. Without people like you, these organisations would not be able to thrive. You purposefully and knowingly broke the laws of this country and, even worse, you showed a callous disregard for the mental health of your own daughter whom the laws were designed to protect. Yours is not a victimless crime. I sentence you to five years in prison."

The Court hadn't even taken a statement from her and they were using her pain to justify his imprisonment. Gini's eyes met her father's across the courtroom. She couldn't stand the guilt she saw there, but she wouldn't look away. He was so frail already. There was every chance he wouldn't make it through five years in jail.

"I love you," she mouthed silently to him and her brother, hoping they would see the words despite what seemed like a vast space between them.

Her brother winked in response, just like he used to when they had played a prank as kids and were about to get in big trouble.

"George Wright, you plead guilty to aiding and abetting your father. You had the power to stop this crime from ever occurring, and you chose not to. I sentence you to three years in prison."

Gini's head dropped then. Three years. Long enough to make travel to any other country impossible. Her brother had channelled his pain at their mother's passing into the international charities he volunteered for. He had lost that outlet forever.

Palmer pulled her to her feet again as the judge left, and she watched her family being herded out by guards like they were criminals.

"We need to wait until the press is gone. I shouldn't have let you come. I'm sorry," Palmer said.

His voice was shaking with nerves and he wouldn't look her in the eye. Gini resisted the urge to slap him. All he could think about was her stupid cover being blown. Who cared about that now? Her family's lives were ruined.

She felt her burner phone vibrate in her pocket and risked checking it while Palmer was distracted looking behind them at the photographers.

I saw what happened on the news. I'm here for you, the text from Jonas said.

Gini couldn't even bring herself to care anymore that he must have listened in to her conversation with Palmer this morning.

I'll come over later, she replied.

It was over an hour before Gini and Palmer could sneak out a side entrance from the court away from the watching media.

"I'll drive you home," Palmer said.

"I'd rather walk."

"It's safer if I drive you. No chance of a stray journalist recognising you."

"It's safer if I'm not seen with you. Piss off."

Palmer grabbed her shoulder and pulled her around to face him.

"Stop pulling that crap. Are you OK? Do you need to pull out of the operation? The Captain will understand."

"So my career can go up in flames, too?" Gini said, her voice flat and emotionless.

Palmer's expression softened. "Take a few days and then we'll talk. You're not thinking straight. There's no way you'll get out of a psych evaluation this time."

Gini blanched. She couldn't protect Jonas if she was taken off the operation.

"This is all I've got left," she muttered.

"We'll figure something out."

Gini shrugged and turned away. Palmer let her go. It wasn't long before she noticed a blue sedan trailing behind her; far enough back that Palmer thought she wouldn't notice. She kept her eyes forward and ignored him.

CHAPTER 6

Gini took the stairs to her apartment two at a time.
She poured herself a drink as soon as she walked in the
door and stared around the room vacantly trying to
process what happened. Her eyes settled on the drawer
where she'd put the illegal reader. She fetched it out
and collapsed on the couch holding it in her hands. It
was deceptively light; its rounded corners belying the
stabbing pain it had caused her.

She couldn't face reading her mother's words again.
Instead, she pulled up the text entry function and
stared at the blinking cursor on the blank screen. She'd
never tried to write anything before, and she didn't
know where to start. She didn't want to rhyme like the
slam poets and she didn't know how to make up
characters like her mother had. But she needed to get
the words out of herself; to bleed some of the pressure
inside her away.

"Screw it," she said to the empty apartment. And
she began to write.

*This is my story. It is a true story, and it is a wake-up call
to the world. If you choose to stay asleep after you read it, that's
on you.*

She stared at the words she had written, reading them over and over. She deleted them and started again.

When I was young, I would have nightmares of monsters. My mother would come hold me in the middle of the night, and pick up the story wherever my dream had left it. Her voice would fill the darkness with comfort. Her words would carry me to safety. Sometimes the monsters would be vanquished, but more often they would be redeemed. Someone would hold up a figurative mirror, and the monster would see the pain that they had caused. They would change. They would grow. That's what people do if they are given the chance.

Gini lost herself in the words she was writing. When she finally looked up from the screen, she had a thousand words or more. She sat steeping in despair. She needed Jonas.

She got changed, and turned her lights and television on so anyone watching her window would think she was still there. She turned her work phone off and slipped out to the rooftop. Palmer would assume she was drinking herself to sleep on her couch. Hopefully, he knew better than to try and visit to comfort her. She pulled her hat down low to conceal her face as she walked towards Jonas's apartment.

When she reached the corner of his block, she paused to watch the people on the street. At least one kept glancing at his building. He could be one of

Jonas's people or he could be another undercover officer. There was no way to know.

Gini looked around and saw a rubbish truck making its halting way down the street. She used it to screen her from view, before ducking down the alleyway to the building's fire escape. By the time the truck was pulling past the alley, she was already levering Jonas's window up to swing herself inside.

She froze at the sound of a soft click from nearby. Her body was hunched forwards and one foot was straddling each side of the window frame.

"Gini! I almost shot you!"

She looked over and saw Jonas putting a gun down on a side table. She never would have heard the bullet coming. She opened her mouth to reply, but no sound came out. Whatever had carried her this far was giving way and it was all she could do not to collapse to the floor.

Jonas crossed the space between them and pulled her into the room and his arms. They were still standing like that when the door crashed open and a man barrelled towards them. Gini tried to pull out of Jonas's arms, but he just held her tighter.

"It's OK, Pete. I knew she was coming. I just thought she'd knock first," he said.

The man stopped just short of them and looked a little sheepish. Gini recognised him as one of the whiskey-drinkers from the pub the other night.

"You were the one watching the apartment on the street. I wasn't sure who you were working for," she said to him.

He frowned and sighed. "I guess I need to work on my surveillance technique."

"I guess we both do. You guys spotted me as soon as I came into the bar," she said.

"Drink?" Jonas asked them, unwrapping his arms from around Gini.

"Doesn't he need to get back to his post?"

"Nah. There's two more outside. Count me in," Pete said, settling himself at the dining table.

Gini watched him warily, guessing he must be more than just a sentry. She trusted Jonas, but she didn't know anything about Pete. He pulled the chair out next to him and gestured for her to join him. She stayed standing. Jonas was returning from the kitchen with three glasses of whiskey. He put them down and came around the table to stand in front of her.

"You can trust us and we can help you, I think. If you want us to. There's never been a better time to push for change. People who've never protested before are already questioning what happened to your family."

"You want to use their story for your plans? Use my pain," she said in a flat voice.

Jonas reached out to stroke her arm. "Yes. But it's so we can stop what happened to them ever happening again."

He leaned forward and kissed her gently, and then joined Pete at the table. At least he was honest, Gini thought. She sat down between them.

"What's the plan?" she said.

"How do we know we can trust you? Jonas isn't exactly objective. I'm not putting years of our work into a cop's hands if there's any chance you could turn on us," Pete said. He was watching Jonas as he said it.

Gini looked down at her hands clenched into fists out of sight under the table. Now that she was starting to feel again, the anger was coming in waves every time she thought back to the sentencing.

It had been building since that first night she read her mother's words. It had been personal then, selfish even. Rage that a censorship algorithm had kept her enslaved to her grief and guilt for so long; the sense of betrayal when her fellow officers took her family away.

But sitting there at the table finally processing what had happened that morning, she realised she had been missing the point. She'd been looking for a simple place to lay the blame. It wasn't just the police or the rules programmed into the Librarian's AI. It was everything. The whole system.

It was the politicians who thought they could control people's thoughts; people who they were supposed to represent. It was the partisan judges that had lost sight of what was just. It was a population of people in denial about what they had lost; who didn't care because they didn't personally feel the pain, her pain. Thirteen other people's lives had been destroyed that morning, and many more would follow if nothing changed.

Gini raised her eyes to look at Pete. Nothing she could say was going to convince him she was trustworthy. There was only one thing that might. She took the illegal reader from her pocket and opened the file she had been writing. She pushed it into the middle of the table.

"Read that. I'm done with the police and this whole shitty system," she said.

She couldn't watch them read it. She didn't want to see their faces. She didn't want to see their pity. She hadn't held anything back in what she wrote—all her pain and anger laid bare in excruciating honesty. She may as well have cut her stomach open and poured her organs out onto the table.

She shoved her chair back and went to sit on the couch with her knees curled up to hide the room from view. She heard a chair leg drag on the floor as someone shifted around the table so they could both read. She felt the heat of her breath as it hit her jeans where her face was buried.

She forced herself to slow her breathing down—four counts in, hold for seven, eight counts out. The only practical technique she'd ever got from mandatory counselling; useful when you needed to focus to take a long-range shot. She wasn't going to lose it in front of them.

She heard murmuring voices, too low to make out, and then the door opening and closing. She still didn't look up. Jonas sat down next to her and held her tight against him, kissing her head.

"Pete's gone. He trusts you. I love you," Jonas said. Each sentence enunciated in the same matter-of-fact way.

Gini turned her face towards him, still curled tight around herself. "Because I'm broken and I hate the world?" she whispered.

That's why Palmer had loved her. She was a project to fix. Someone to make him feel needed. Not that he would have put it like that.

"Because you're strong. Because you're willing to learn and change your mind. Because you see a problem so big most people would give up and you say 'what's the plan?'. Because I can't be anything but exactly myself with you, even when I'm supposed to hide who I am, and I think you might be the same," Jonas said.

He drew back a little and waited for her response. Gini sat and tried to figure out if the person she'd pretended to be for him was actually her. Virginia Wright didn't open up to people. That wasn't who she was. But maybe that wasn't the point. Maybe the point was that she could have told him anything when she pretended to be the kind of person that shared her feelings, but she'd told him the truth. She hadn't even managed to keep her name a secret. He was right. Even when she was pretending to be Kat, she'd been exactly herself.

She wished she could make herself say something as heartfelt as he had in reply, but that was never going to happen. Instead, she unfurled her body and reached out to kiss him. She felt his mouth curl into a smile for a moment before he kissed her back. He got it. He got her.

The light from the streetlamps was shining through the window by the time they left the couch.

"So, what's the plan?" Gini asked for the second time.

"We have a piece of code. A virus, of sorts, created by the original programmer of the Librarian AI when she realised where things were heading. We've been working to find a way to spread it across the reader network."

"What does it do?"

"She called it 'Mary Sue'. It basically tells your reader that you're perfect in every way. No past trauma, no violent or depressive tendencies, no criminal or political 'radicalist' past to trigger censorship."

"Will that make any difference?"

"It's a start. People will begin to realise what they're missing. The censorship criteria have been expanding exponentially for the last couple of years without most people noticing. My organisation will release a lot of government information while the virus is active, so it doesn't get restricted. Stories of people like you. We can't force change. People have to want it. People have to fight for it. It will take time."

"So, how do you get the virus out there?" Gini asked.

"That's where you come in. The new laws give the police access to every reader in the country without a warrant to 'monitor biometric data that could reveal a crime'. Any computer in cyber-crimes will be able to access it. All we have to do is load the program and run a nationwide reader-search. The virus will do the rest."

Gini gritted her teeth in frustration. "I don't even have access at the moment. I'm on stress-leave until I pass a psych evaluation."

Jonas paused and seemed to choose his words carefully.

"Detective Palmer seems to have a… weakness… for you. Can we use that? We need to strike while people are still reeling from the court case. In a few days, they'll have moved on."

Gini forced herself to count her breathing again, fighting not to lose her temper.

"What exactly are you suggesting I do? Sleep with him? That's not going to make him break protocol to let me search the system."

"That's not what I meant! Do you really think I'd want that?" Jonas looked hurt.

Gini looked away, guilt replacing anger. "No. Sorry. Let me think."

She walked to the dining table and pushed at the reader she'd left there. The only reader in the country that contained the words she'd written. A plan started forming in her mind. She looked up at Jonas.

"What if I tell him your organisation is communicating through reader-to-reader coded messages? I could say the key-phrase changes every week with the slam themes. We can search the network for lines from the last slam. There should be plenty of readers with some of that poetry on them. They'll be chasing down leads for months."

Jonas was nodding. "That could work, but he might get suspicious at so many hits. Let's put a dummy phrase on this reader and say you stole it. I'll get my people to plant readers with matching phrases around town. See if we can't sneak some into the houses of those politicians that voted for the legislative reform.

That should keep them busy accusing each other while we relocate. It won't be safe to stay here. Give me a couple of hours and we should be sorted."

"If I manage to get out. I'll disappear somewhere safe, too. You better not tell me where you're going, just in case," Gini said, not looking at him.

"Don't be stupid. I'll be waiting outside the station for you. All you have to do is get out of the building and into the car. It's a silver BMW. I'm not leaving you behind."

She glared at him, but she could see he wasn't going to back down. If he got himself caught, she would never forgive herself. Neither of them bothered discussing the fact that Palmer would probably arrest her on the spot when he realised what was happening, anyway.

It only took them a few minutes to cobble together a suitable phrase on her reader and plant the virus code behind it. Jonas kissed Gini long and hard before she climbed out the window to make her way back down the fire escape.

"Make it to that car, Gini. Don't make me come find you," he said.

Gini shrugged. "I'll do my best. Don't get caught with those readers."

The last thing she saw of the apartment was Jonas bent over the table copying the phrase onto every illegal reader he had stashed there while issuing urgent instructions to someone over his phone.

CHAPTER 7

Gini peeked over the edge of the roof when she made it back to her building. It was hard to tell what colour the cars parked by the back entrance were, but she could just make out a slight glow that could be the light of a cell phone coming from one of them.

She made her way down to her apartment and turned her work cell back on while she changed into the black cargo pants and leather jacket she usually wore at the precinct. A little of the tension left her body when she saw she'd only missed one message from Palmer. She had worried he might break her door down while she was out.

I'm here for you if you need me. Sent two hours ago.

She put the whiskey bottle and an empty glass on the table, and double checked the incriminating phone and reader were safely stashed in her pockets. Then she messaged him back.

Literally. Is that you outside my building? Creep.

That might have been a bit harsh, but she couldn't let him get suspicious. He needed to think nothing had changed. She poured herself a drink and waited. He was nothing if not predictable. She'd barely drunk half when he rapped on the door. She rubbed her eyes hard to make them look red and then opened it, whiskey still in hand.

"What do you want?" she said.

His eyes flicked from her face to the drink and back. "To help you, Gin. Stop pushing away the only friend you've got."

She stared at him and counted her breaths again as if she was trying to decide whether to trust him. Luring him in.

"I've got a lead. It's big," she said, finally.

"Great! How? When?"

"On Saturday, before… I needed to leave. I stole a reader from one of my marks."

"Gin! You didn't have a warrant! What the hell?"

"It's got a code-phrase on it we can use to trace the whole operation, but we need to search for it now before they change it. The warrant doesn't matter. We won't have to use the reader in court. We can just use it to identify the people to surveille," Gini said.

Palmer still looked dubious but he was calming down as he realised they could fudge it so it didn't undermine the whole operation.

"And you think you might be able to avoid the psych eval if you get a major breakthrough," he said, knowingly. "What exactly are we searching?"

"The reader network. They're using it to communicate. We can access the whole country, no warrant needed."

Palmer was nodding. "OK. That might work. We can try anyway. I'll take the reader in tonight and do the search."

"I'm not letting you take all the credit for this. Besides, there might be another layer of security I need to crack. I know these people better than you do. I need to be there. I need to stop them from luring innocent people to prison ever again," Gini said.

She thought she might have laid it on too thick, but Palmer was lapping it up. He reached out to hold her shoulder with an understanding expression on his face.

"You don't even have access to the building, Gin," Palmer said.

Gini stared at him until he looked away. "I'm not giving you the reader if you don't take me with you."

Palmer sighed. "Fine. Have it your way. You always do. We'll go after shift change. There are fewer people to recognise you on graveyard."

"I'll meet you outside in two hours," Gini said.

Then she shut the door on him. The less time she spent with him, the less chance he'd realise something was wrong.

She messaged Jonas while she waited. *Palmer agreed. Heading to the station at midnight.*

We'll be ready. I'll be at the side entrance on 3rd Street. Don't do anything stupid, he messaged back.

Palmer jumped in his seat when Gini knocked on his car window two hours later.

"One day you're going to sneak up on the wrong person and get shot," he said as she got in the car.

"Not if I shoot them first."

Palmer rolled his eyes and started the car.

"Are we going to talk about what happened this morning?" he said.

"Nothing to say. They were caught committing a crime. The judge sentenced them."

"You know I can see through that act, right?" Palmer said.

He reached out and squeezed her hand as he drove. Gini's body went stiff and she froze until he took his hand away.

"Was I really that bad?" he said, so softly she almost didn't hear him.

Gini looked out the window. She needed to shut this down before it messed up the whole plan.

"No. You're not that bad. You just always push. I need to work things through in my own time, not yours."

"Wow. That was… unexpectedly honest." He sounded impressed.

Gini kept her eyes trained on the city-scape passing by, the streetlights turning the structures sepia in the darkness like they were travelling through some old-time cop movie.

103

"Just because I don't talk about my feelings, doesn't mean I'm not dealing with them."

"Point taken."

They pulled into the precinct car park. Gini looked around for a silver BMW, but she was on the wrong side of the building anyway. Her mind started planning escape routes in case Jonas didn't show.

The desk sergeant looked up as they came in. "Detective Palmer. Can I help you? She's not supposed to be here."

Gini kept her face neutral and placed one hand on the reader in her pocket.

"I need her help sorting some paperwork before the captain looks over it tomorrow," Palmer said.

The sergeant grinned and shook his head. "Get behind again, Palmer? Alright. You better keep an eye on her though."

Gini opened her mouth to insult him and Palmer pulled her away down the corridor.

"Leave it, Gin."

"I'm not a damn baby."

"Stop acting like one then."

Gini glared at him and forced herself to keep walking. They were in. That was what mattered. The sooner she could leave this place forever, the better. Palmer sat down at the computer and logged in.

"We have to transfer the file across so the decryption key goes with it. Let me do it," Gini said.

She pulled up the search and synched the reader, careful to keep the adrenaline tremor in her hands under control. The transfer hung from the size of the hidden virus and Gini turned to Palmer to distract him, hoping he wouldn't notice.

"Thanks for doing this. I really appreciate it. I just need to know what happened to my family won't happen again. I need to shut it all down," she said. The truth was always more convincing.

He raised his eyebrows. "You're welcome. You really are changing. We can get through this," he said, reaching out to squeeze her hand again.

Gini resisted the urge to pull away and turned back to the computer as the notification popped up that the file had loaded. She set the search going and leaned back in the chair.

"Now we just wait. I'll start an email to the Captain explaining, and a list of the addresses as we get the hits," she said, pulling up another window.

The search had already found the first of Jonas's planted readers and marked it as a red dot on a map of the city. She copied the address across and started crafting a sufficiently convincing email for the Captain. She was so focused on writing that she didn't notice Palmer's silence. Another three addresses had been flagged before she thought to look over at him.

Panic stabbed through her as she saw he was engrossed in the reader; his eyes scanning across the screen obsessively. She hadn't locked it. There was only one thing on it that would have distracted him from the search—her writing.

"Gini, I'm so sorry. I never realised you felt like this," he said, as he looked up from the reader.

She stared at him in horror. It was one thing to bare her soul to Jonas and his criminal partner. She had never meant for it to be read by bloody Palmer. Partly because he was so insufferable, and partly because she didn't want his do-gooder self to go to jail when this whole thing blew up.

She did the only thing she could think of. She spun around in her chair and snapped out a punch that knocked him out cold before he'd even had a chance to register what was happening.

The search had broadened well beyond the city now, spreading the virus with it. She locked the screen and left it going. Hopefully, it would be enough. She couldn't stick around any longer to find out. She grabbed Palmer's gun and the reader, pausing to check he was breathing OK. She hoped the concussion wasn't too bad. With any luck, he'd have short-term memory loss and wouldn't be able to remember reading her story.

She messaged Jonas before she left the room. *Coming now. Search on track. Committed assault. You'd better be waiting.*

She forced herself to walk calmly down the hallways towards the side exit. She nodded to the desk sergeant having a coffee on his break as she passed the kitchen.

"Where's Palmer? Are you done with your paperwork?" he called out.

"Palmer's a pain in the arse. He can do it without me," she snapped.

The Sergeant smirked and went back to his coffee. It was exactly the sort of reaction he expected from her. She knew she only had a matter of minutes before he went to check on Palmer, though. She was supposed to be supervised.

She broke into a jog once she was out of sight. No time to mess around, now. If the station went into lock-down, she was screwed. She could see the exit up ahead. She was almost there.

"Wright? What are doing here?" Detective Jennings called from behind her.

He wasn't supposed to be on duty. She knew because they'd checked the duty roster before they came. He must have been called in. Someone had raised the alarm. She kept walking, ignoring him. She was four steps away from the door.

"Wright, freeze! I have my gun out. Don't make me shoot you."

She stopped where she was, one hand touching the door handle.

"Are you behind this hack? You trying to get back at us for your family?"

"I'm not trying to get back at anyone," she said.

"Take your hand out of your pocket. Slowly."

Gini turned to face him, opening the door a little as she did and wedging her heel against it to keep it in place. Her other hand was still in her pocket, feeling the smooth cold surface of Palmer's gun. She could shoot Jennings right now. He'd never see it coming. He'd probably shoot her, too. There wouldn't be any jail then. She could be free of it all. She'd done her bit.

She felt her phone vibrate against her leg. Jonas's reply. Jonas who was waiting outside and would probably be caught in whatever cross-fire she started. She wasn't her mother. She wasn't going to make the same mistakes. Her eyes caught a flicker of motion and she saw Palmer staggering down the hallway towards them. She watched him look from Jennings to her and back again.

"Who's there? Someone attacked me. I can't see properly," he called out.

"It's Detective Jennings. Hold your position, Palmer. I've apprehended Wright."

Palmer had almost reached him. Gini took her hand out of her pocket. She couldn't risk shooting him. She held both hands palm-outwards towards the two men. Then she blinked in surprise. Palmer was holding three fingers up just out of Jennings field of vision. Then two. Then one.

"I can't see you, Detective. You're all blurry. Where are you?" he said, stumbling into Jennings.

There wouldn't be another chance. Gini ripped the door open as the sound of Jennings' firearm discharging ricocheted around the hallway. That's what happens when you tackle someone pointing a gun at someone. Stupid Palmer and his stupid need to save her. He wasn't just going to get himself fired, he was going to get killed.

She was pulling the door shut behind her and running down the street before she felt the wetness running down her arm and realised it wasn't Palmer that had copped the bullet. Jennings had caught her in the shoulder. She swore.

For a panicked moment, she searched the empty street for a car. Then she heard the sound of an engine coming up behind her and spun around—a silver BMW. She yanked the door open and collapsed into the front seat as Jonas pulled away.

"You did it! The virus is still spreading. It's already gone far enough to make a difference. Our people are releasing the information. They won't be able to shut it down in time," Jonas said.

"That's nice," Gini said.

Her head was spinning and the darkness of the car seemed to be seeping into her brain. Jonas looked over at her in alarm.

"Gini? Shit! What happened?" Jonas slammed on the brakes.

"Got shot. Don't stop. I'll be fine."

Jonas grabbed a scarf from the back seat and wrapped it tight around her shoulder.

"No time. Drive," she said, pushing him away as the pain surged again.

He cursed and accelerated. They could hear sirens in the distance. There was no way to tell if their vehicle had been identified or not. Nothing to do but keep driving.

Gini pulled the reader out and opened the file of her writing. Then she fished a business card out of her pocket—Deanna Myers, the reporter from the trial. Before she could reconsider, she emailed it through to her. She'd never meant to share what she'd written, but they could be caught or killed at any moment. The words had convinced Palmer she was worth helping. Maybe they'd help tip the balance with the rest of the country, too.

Gini reached out and squeezed Jonas's hand where it rested on the gearshift.

If you enjoyed *Would She Be Gone*, you can purchase the sequel, *Compact of Fire* on Amazon or online.

A SQUASH OF COMMUTERS

First published in *Apocalypse* from Black Hare Press
in December 2019

A squash of peak-hour commuters sit in a train carriage. They would be a mob of commuters if they were moving under their own propulsion. Or a pride of commuters if they had better green credentials.

When the ocean floods the underground, they become a pod. And when they emerge from the dark to a post-apocalyptic future they become a colony.

The underground tunnels protected them from the worst of it. As the years pass and the population dwindles, they look back on the days when they were a squash with longing.

A scarcity of commuters is all that remains.

A NEW COLD WAR

First published in *Daily Science Fiction* in April 2019

Sarah glanced up at the TV above the bar and saw a red 'breaking news' banner appear at the bottom of the screen. She called out to the bartender to turn it up.

The head of the Security Council was holding a press conference. "Today, we have learned of the greatest threat humanity has ever faced…"

She sat back in her chair and raised a hand to her mouth. It had worked. It had really worked. She was so shocked she couldn't even listen and realised she'd missed half the statement. She leaned forward ignoring the way her elbows stuck to the table in the dingy bar and forced herself to concentrate.

"Effective immediately, we are introducing severe restrictions and sinking caps on fossil fuel usage. We expect our allies to support these measures. This is a matter of global security. Legislation is being passed under urgency to introduce sanctions for any breaches. Our military budgets will be redirected to replacement technologies as a matter of priority. We will be working with the largest contributors first and carefully monitoring results. If those measures are unsuccessful, we will have to severely restrict any non-essential travel using fossil fuel combustion engines."

The speaker paused in his speech and the camera zoomed in to watch him look down and take a shaking breath. Then his head raised and he stared right down the barrel of the lens. "These creatures are threatening our very existence. We need every citizen of the world, every business, every Government to do their bit to drive them back to where they came from. We can all be heroes in this fight. We will not go gentle into the hot night!"

When Sarah got back to her hotel room, a woman who'd asked pointed questions during her presentation earlier in the day was waiting by the door, talking on her phone.

Sarah stopped searching for her key card, hand paused halfway into her purse. She could feel panicked heat rising in her face.

The woman hung up her phone and looked at her for a long moment.

"Don't worry, I just want to talk. These guys will wait outside," she said, gesturing to her security detail standing partway down the hall in both directions.

Sarah couldn't do anything but open the door and let her in. She wondered if it was all about to come crashing down before it even started.

The door shut behind them with a bang and the woman walked straight to the minibar and found a bottle of whiskey. She poured them two glasses neat and sat down at the table. She waited till Sarah collapsed into the opposite chair before she started talking.

"I'm not a scientist, but I like to think I know my way around evidence. Today is the first time I can ever recall my science advisor not giving me a lecture about correlation versus causation when faced with data like yours."

Sarah stared at her face looking for a hint of what she wanted, but it didn't give anything away. "Well, the data builds on the foundation of consensus that has emerged in climate science in recent years. While the premise may seem alien, the data is very robust."

Sara winced at the pun as soon as it left her mouth. She wished she hadn't gone to the bar. She needed to be more careful. The woman looked down into her drink, contemplating the amber swirling liquid. She didn't look up when she spoke.

"If we take away the 'invisible alien premise' for a minute. Could you tell me truthfully – are the temperatures and timeframes accurate?"

"Yes, completely accurate," she said. The strain was starting to show in her voice.

The woman nodded to herself. "And the scientific community, specifically all of the science advisors at the presentation today, they agree with the interpretation of the data on those points?"

"They do," Sarah said.

"And you know this because you had spoken with them beforehand, yes?" she asked.

"Yes," Sarah said again. A bead of sweat trickled down her side. She hadn't meant to admit that.

They had wondered how many leaders would question the science. They'd used the latest behavioural psychology and persuasion research to shape the presentation, but the debate had raged on whether the risk to the reputation of the scientific method was worth it. It was actually the insights of the security council science advisors that had finally won the day. They had been confident that the leaders who were smart enough to understand the science were smart enough to understand that this may be earth's last chance. The sunk cost fallacy and political pragmatism should be strong enough to hold them all to the course of action once a commitment was made. The risk was all in these early days.

The silence stretched across the cheap Formica hotel table. Sara could see the woman working through the moral dilemma in her mind, just like she had. She could almost feel the strain of the ethical gymnastics she was forcing on her.

Finally, the woman leaned back in her seat and looked up at her again. "I'm impressed. I've never seen them agree on anything."

Sara took advantage of the sliver of hope she was offering. "When the future of humanity is at stake you'd hope that people would put their differences aside and do what's needed. The stakes are the same with or without the alien premise," she said.

The woman knocked back her whiskey in one hit and slammed it down on the table. "I guess we'd better go starve some malevolent gas-based life forms then. A cold war for our generation."

Sara raised her glass. "A new cold war."

LIVE UNDERGROUND

First published on Twitter in December 2018

Live underground.
Wait for the day the earth is fully habitable.
Dream of swapping rations for a crisp apple,
and tears for pH neutral rain.

Melanie Harding-Shaw
@MelHardingShaw

Live underground.
Wait for the day the earth is fully habitable.
Dream of swapping rations for a crisp apple,
and tears for pH neutral rain.
#rāmereshorts #vss365

9:45 AM · Dec 7, 2018 · Twitter Web Client

GAC ATG ATT ACA

First published in *Little Blue Marble* in December 2019

Erika liked to think of herself as a gene artist. That was how she kept the despair at bay in the claustrophobic bunker deep under the ground. She had never stood on the earth's surface; neither had her mother, grandmother, or many generations before them.

Instead, she worked to keep the gene pool viable in the small population here. She carefully designed each new baby and recorded their genome in the computer for future geneticists to reference. In her lifetime she had added two generations to the records. Current estimates were that short trips to the surface may finally be possible in three years. She might live that long—just.

She'd discovered the code in the notebooks of her predecessor when she first started working. She had relished the challenge of sequencing a genetically viable child that also contained a message for future generations. Once she knew what to look for it was time-consuming, but not complicated, to find the line in each person's DNA that contained the message.

The texts were all short—only a single sentence per person. It had taken her a year to realise that she could follow the messages down generations of a family to create a longer work. A poem. Art.

Some families' genes contained descriptions of the world, told through the words of changing gene artists who had all felt the same despair:

The sky is just a story now.
Walls close in around us.
Hope is for the future.
We exist always in today.

Sometimes the messages were more personal and stood alone. There wasn't space for everyone who wanted a child to have one:

I am the treasured culmination of a generation of longing.

Erika had thought about telling her replacement the secret of the code, but she hadn't wanted to deny him the excitement of the discovery in their unchanging world. Now she spent her twilight years looking back through the records, assembling and reassembling their poems. She looked right back to the first postapocalyptic generations.

Toxicity levels on the surface were one year from dropping to safe levels when she came across the records of an early family line that had not continued. The notes said they had sacrificed their own procreation rights so another couple could have a child. Their poetry had been lost to future gene artists. There were only two generations recorded:

We are not alone in the world, I will find the others.

Latitude -41.28664, Longitude 174.77557

Erika stared at the screen and started to cry. She had never dared to believe that another outpost of humanity might exist. Every child of the bunker was raised with stories of the people who had tried to leave and died from exposure to the harsh and toxic surface world. It didn't stop a handful trying every generation and breaking the hearts of those left behind. She could understand why someone would hide this information.

She looked up the geneticist who had left the coordinates all those generations ago and then she looked up the code of their only child. It contained the shortest message she'd ever found. So short she almost overlooked it—*GAC ATG ATT ACA*: Hope.

TIME EXPLOSION

First published on Twitter in August 2019.

Time explosion. Yesterdays fly around like shrapnel. A shard of next week lost in my leg on impact. You involve me because I died tomorrow.

 **Melanie Harding-Shaw**
@MelHardingShaw

Time explosion. Yesterdays fly around like shrapnel. A shard of next week lost in my leg on impact. You involve me because I died tomorrow.
#RāmereShorts #VSS365 #SciFiFri

9:49 AM · Aug 16, 2019 · Twitter Web App

IRONY

Not previously published

The need to know consumed me. I had tried questioning my aunts, uncles, grandparents and long-lost cousins. None of them could tell me, or none of them would tell me. The result was the same either way. I had no other option than to make an offering, despite the risks. The god of domestic OCD, ill-gotten gains, and family secrets could be a fickle master.

I knew my family shrine was too small for the scope of knowledge that I sought. A boon so great would require an echo chamber large enough to contain it. So, I googled to find a larger place of worship. There were so few left. As modern technologies advanced, the god had splintered into a billion different faces.

The church I found backed onto an abandoned parking lot. The pews were crusted with stains, an irony that matched the deity's sense of humour. Even the word irony belonged to him—an extension of his spheres.

I was one of the few who still remembered the old ways. A sprig of lavender, a silver coin, and heirloom lace made up my plea. I balanced them on a coin-operated machine full of my family's clothes. From each aunt and uncle I had visited, each grandparent and cousin, I had stolen a single shirt. Now they tumbled in a rainbow behind the machine's glass door. The vibrations shook my bones where I sat on the faded red bench between the sticky residue of spilled fabric softener and a crumb of melted chocolate that had fused with the surface.

Whether it was the vibrations or the stifling humid air I don't know, but I woke an hour later to the insistent tones of the completed cycle. I stretched and stumbled as I rose on legs that had fallen as asleep as the rest of me. When I opened the washing machine, each shirt was neatly folded in a pile with not a sleeve out of place. My hands shook as I transferred the tower of crisply crease-free clothing to my basket. My prayer had been answered.

The day my father left us, I was six. He'd said he was going to get some milk and he never returned. The police had looked at my screaming seven siblings and the piles of dirty washing all around, and smiled with pity when my mother said it must be foul play. They thought he had run away. After ten years, they finally declared him dead. No trace was ever found.

Each time I did a load of washing after that day at the laundromat church, a new memory of his would flash into my mind—the first time my father held me, the time I rode on his shoulders at the fair. As the years passed I saw other things—an ironing board, a man with a broad malevolent smile and knuckles crossed with scars, and my mother. The memories grew more painful—his pain and mine. I could no longer look my mother in the eye.

My children wondered why my clothes were stained and dirty. They offered to wash them for me, but I couldn't risk them seeing what I saw. They grew tired of buying me new things to wear when the smell became overpowering. They stopped coming to visit. There was nothing I could do. I knew there was only one memory left and I could not watch it. I should have listened to my aunts and uncles, to my grandparents. Some things cannot be unseen.

My mother lived to the age of 78. The day after her funeral, a letter arrived from her lawyer. It was addressed in my mother's hand and sealed with blood-red wax. The ink that formed my name was smudged with tears that had long since evaporated.

I placed the clothes I had cleared from my mother's house into the washing machine. I sat down on the cold linoleum laundry floor and stared through the glass door at the crumpled fabric within. My mother's letter rested on my lap. I was still wearing the clothes I had bought for the funeral, and I picked at the residue of someone's spilled coffee on my leg.

My hand shook as I reached out to press the start button on the cycle. I broke the seal on her letter as I heard the water rushing into the steel drum. Her words floated in my mind like subtitles to the silent movie of memories that washed over me. My tears flowed as strong as the water through the hoses feeding the depths of the machine. When the deluge finally abated, the final sentence of her letter hung in the air for a moment—I'm sorry. The beeps of the completed cycle chased them away. It was finally over.

I looked down to see the letter in my hands was sodden and I was sitting in a pool of inky, salty water that had run off the pages. My mother's words were now illegible. I opened the washing machine and found a pile of neatly folded, creaseless clothes. Not my mother's, but the clothes I had worn to the laundromat shrine all those years ago and had long since discarded—a conciliatory farewell from a fickle god. I put them in the trash.

I wondered what cosmic intelligence had even thought to create a single god in charge of washing, money laundering, and the secrets that are a family's dirty laundry; like some epic dad-joke. Did the other gods make fun of him? Whatever. I was done with him. I would never worship him again.

I spent the rest of the day washing every single one of my clothes, twice, but the stains were too deep. I used some of my inheritance from my mother to treat myself to a new wardrobe. None of us were sure how she'd come by so much money, but it had been a relief not to worry about finances while we were mourning. Then I reached out to my estranged children. Not to tell them what happened, of course. Some secrets are too painful to reveal.

BREAK GLASS IN CASE OF EMERGENCY

First published in *Curses & Cauldrons* from Blood Song Books in August 2019

The ability to fly was nothing special in space. She was just an archaic failsafe in case the engineers' spacesuit propulsion failed. Her broom was stored in a case by the hangar door. *Break glass in case of emergency.* As if anyone else could make it fly. They thought it funny to allocate her to the cleaning crew maintaining sweeping bots.

She watched fiery spells twist around the Captain's neck when the alien attack came. The sound of breaking glass chimed like faerie music in her ears. She never looked back as she joined her inter-galactic cousins in the stars.

COMMON DENOMINATOR

First published in *Wild Musette Journal* in October 2018

Reprinted in *Year's Best Aotearoa New Zealand Science Fiction and Fantasy Volume 1*

When I first met my latest ex, 'Sultans of Swing' by Dire Straits was belting out of the speakers and I had to wipe my hands before I danced with him because the bar was so sticky from spilled beer. That dance set up a false expectation for our relationship, although the bar itself should have tipped me off. I wonder what my chip would have played that night if I'd had it back then. Maybe 'Luka' by Suzanne Vega.

He was just the latest in a series of poor choices on my part. Each time, I swear that the next time will be different. But it never is – I don't know how to be different. I am the common denominator in my relationships. Maybe they're my own fault.

When they asked for volunteers to beta test a media chip implanted in your brain I was first in line, although the queue wasn't exactly stretching around the block. The promise of music played directly to my auditory cortex in response to my emotions was too tempting to refuse. I don't deserve much but I had always known my messed-up life deserved its own soundtrack.

The chip didn't disappoint. When I was depressed, it played something I couldn't help but dance to. When I was angry, it mellowed me out. Soon everybody with money had one. I would never have been able to afford one myself.

I was sitting at a bar the first time it happened. A guy came and leaned beside me. He was wearing a white-collared shirt with the top two buttons undone so I had to keep pulling my eyes back up to his face and he smelled like clean clothes and money. He was looking at the chip controller on my wrist.

"You don't see many of those around here," he said with a smooth smile. He pulled his sleeve up a little and put his wrist next to mine to compare. "Yours looks like a newer model." His fingers brushed mine as he pulled his sleeve back down.

I smiled into his blue eyes, "Yeah, I'm a tester. This upgrade hasn't been released yet." I would have carried on, maybe asked him to dance, but 'Smooth Criminal' by Michael Jackson started playing in my mind so loud that it drowned out every other sound in the bar. I winced and rubbed my temples and the volume went down a little.

"Are you OK? Can I buy you a drink?" the guy asked.

Was I OK? I wasn't sure. The chip was not supposed to do that. "No thanks, I need to go sorry." I grabbed my coat from the stool next to me.

"Here's my card. Give me a call when you're feeling better," he said. As he helped me put my coat on, his hands ran down my arms and I trembled a little. Was I being silly? The chip was designed to respond to my emotions and the only thing I was feeling was horny, it must be defective. He was beautiful and clearly successful. He was nothing like my ex-boyfriends. The volume of 'Smooth Criminal' went back up. The common denominator in my relationships is me. I left without him.

I had to report the incident to the developers of course. Playing loud music while you're at a bar listening to loud music is not what the chips are supposed to do. I knew something was wrong when they didn't let me leave. Instead I was interviewed by progressively more and more senior people at the company. No-one was telling me what was going on, but I could kind of tell what the problem was. "Were your controllers still touching when the music started? Did they try and synch with each other?"

No, they didn't, not that I noticed anyway. But I guess my chip was reading something from his chip or they wouldn't be asking. When I finally got home I trawled the internet for anything about the guy. He was a high-flying investment banker. I used the email address on his card to find his Facebook page, wondering if I should send him a friend request just to get access. His privacy settings were locked right down and everything else was corporate vanilla.

A folk guitar intro started playing in my mind and I looked down at my controller in surprise – 'Whisper Your Mother's Name' by Jimmie Rodgers. I hit the stop button, it really wasn't my thing. The chip was definitely defective. As soon as I took my hand away it started playing again. My finger hovered over the stop button. Would the developers have been so worried if it was just a defect though?

I looked again at the Facebook login screen in front of me and then touched the back of my neck where the chip had been implanted with shaking hands. It only took a moment of searching his friends list to figure out who his mother was. I typed her name into the password field and was rewarded with full access to his page and messages.

He was too clever to put anything incriminating on Facebook messenger but the signs were clear for someone with my history. He looked different to my exes on the outside, but inside he was just the same. He was an abusive predator and he had at least three women on the hook.

The developers left me five messages the next day asking me to come in and have the chip removed. I looked around my dirty apartment, breathed in the smog from the diesel trains that ran below my window, and I packed a bag and left. 'Cold War' by Janelle Monae was the soundtrack of my escape. Was I alone?

I am the common denominator in my relationships. That is my super power. I'm not a victim any more. The chip and I can tell if you're going to beat me, or worse. Together, we can do something about it.

ONLY CHILD

First published in *Takahē* in April 2020

I always wondered why my parents liked my brother more than me when they were so lucky to have me. Why he never got in trouble, even that time he stole my favourite book and dropped it in the pool.

It was the day he dropped my best friend in the pool that I understood. I pushed him into the water in retaliation. He turned the pool live and electrocuted my friend.

My parents thought an android brother would teach me empathy. Five minutes with a hairdryer and he was good as new. We never did tell them what happened.

REVOLUTIONS

First published in *New Orbit* in October 2018

Eve sat in the front seat of the car with her legs turned away from her husband. She was slightly curled into herself as if that might have any effect at all on the pain. When she could do more than just cope again, she looked out her window at the neglected fence posts leaning down the steep slope on the side of the road.

The wind turbines in the distance echoed the revolutions of the wheels of the car beneath her. When the wind blew too hard the engineers let the turbines stand still so they didn't get damaged. Labour was not so forgiving. Even with all the advances in modern medicine, no-one had thought to invent a pause button to let women avoid getting damaged.

They had left for hospital earlier in the process than most expectant parents because they knew the trip to the city would take time. Eve felt the pain of a contraction starting again and did her best not to get angry at her husband for ignoring her pleas for a self-driving car. He could have been holding her and supporting her right now. She could have had enough space to stretch out. He'd said they couldn't afford to spend the money with a new baby on the way, but she knew the real reason was his love of driving. She couldn't really complain though; that was why he'd agreed to live in the beautiful rural area they now called home.

Kyle gripped the steering wheel with white knuckles and did his best to keep the car under the speed limit as he listened to the noises of pain coming from his wife next to him. He tried to estimate the number of minutes between her contractions. Before they'd left he'd reminded her to keep entering the times into the hospital app that their midwife would be monitoring. She'd gestured rudely at him and told him to do it himself before she went back to hanging on to the doorframe. The car crossed the centre line a little as he took a corner on the winding road too fast and Eve cried out in pain.

"Slow down! That makes it worse!" she said, in between panting breaths. She was starting to hyperventilate.

"Sorry, Love. I'm just worried we left it too late. How often are your contractions coming?" he replied.

"Too often," was all she said.

They had reached the highway, 10 minutes' drive from the hospital on a good day, when they hit the traffic jam. Stopped cars stretched before them like some sort of metallic ocean. Kyle watched the dial on his dashboard drop to zero as he braked. He checked his phone. There had been a multiple-fatality accident ahead. Estimated delay – 1 hour.

The self-driving car in front of him backed up to within an inch of his front bumper and started a series of turns to make its way to a nearby small gap in the median barrier. Other self-driving cars were shifting in the same way, programmed to communicate with each other. They worked together to get as many of them as possible out of the traffic. One by one they slipped through the narrow gap to make a U-turn on the highway.

Kyle pounded the steering wheel with a fist. He would have risked the large fine for human-driven cars changing direction on the highway, but there was no way that he could even get close to the gap.

Five cars ahead he could see a driverless car start flashing red. The occupants must have hit their emergency priority button, probably just in frustration at their inability to get out of the traffic. The drivers in front of him started tooting their horns as their reverse lights came on. If they were too slow responding to the priority beacon the car would lodge a complaint. The reversing beeps of his car seemed to mock him. Kyle backed his car up, begrudging even that small movement further away from where he needed to be. He watched in frustration as the flashing car extracted itself from the sea of metal and sped off in the other direction.

Five minutes later, Eve's moans had turned into screams. Kyle had started entering the contraction times into the hospital app now that they were stopped. He didn't know what else to do. He'd assumed his wife would run things until they got to the hospital. He'd just entered the latest time – 2 minutes – when the phone started ringing; it was the midwife.

"Kyle, those contractions are progressing really quickly. Where are you?"

"We're stuck on the highway."

"Why didn't you… never mind. I'm calling you an ambulance right now. I need to talk to Eve."

Kyle waited for Eve's latest scream to subside and then put the phone on speaker.

"Eve, it's Michelle. You're doing really well. I need you to tell me what you're feeling."

"It hurts so much. I don't think I can do this."

"You can do it Eve, but I need you to keep talking to me. The ambulance is twenty minutes away. Is there anything else you can tell me about how you're feeling?"

Eve started screaming again and Kyle felt panic set in. He tried to put an arm around her but she pushed him away and clutched tight to the armrest instead. Through her window he could see the face of a child in the neighbouring car staring back at him with wide eyes. He turned and looked out behind them while Eve was distracted. Every self-driving car that hadn't managed to make it out of the traffic jam yet was glowing red to help clear a path for the ambulance to come through. They only did that in emergencies. If there had been more of them they would have looked like an airport runway, but instead they looked like lonely signal lights in a vast ocean.

"Can't the ambulance come from the other direction?" he asked Michelle in panic.

"Traffic's backed up just the same on the other side, Kyle. You'll be OK. I'm right here for you and I've got an open line to emergency services. Eve, just keep breathing, in through your nose and out through your mouth. When you can manage, start talking to me again."

Kyle watched in despair as a small trickle of self-driving cars went past in the other direction only three lanes away from him. If something happened to Eve or their baby because he hadn't wanted to borrow money for a new car he didn't think he could live with himself.

Eve's cracking voice came from next to him "I think my waters broke about fifteen minutes ago," she said.

Kyle's eyes widened, "Why didn't you say anything?"

"You were driving, I didn't want to distract you. It's not a big deal." she started breathing fast again and whimpered, feeling another contraction building up.

"It might not mean the baby's coming." Michelle's voice was soft and calming "But when you've already been labouring for a while it can mean it's time to start pushing. Do you have towels with you, Kyle? I think Eve should be sitting in the back with more space just in case."

"I can't do this," Kyle said, just as Eve started screaming again.

She was still moaning loudly when Michelle started talking again. "Kyle, I need you to go put clean towels down in the back seat and move her back there right now. Pick up the phone and open the door. The ambulance is ten minutes away."

Michelle's calm voice had a hypnotic effect on him and he was half out the door already before he even realised. Once he started moving, his brain started trying to function again. He laid everything out in the back and opened his wife's door.

Kyle held tight under Eve's arm and half-pulled her out of the car. The towel they'd put down on the seat stuck to her clothes as she stood up. He reached down to pull it away from her and stared at it for a moment in confusion. There was large dark patch in the middle of the towel that became bright red at the edges like some sort of Rorshach inkblot test. For a moment his brain tried to figure out what animal he could see in the pattern and what that said about him; then he realised what the stain was.

As he was staring at the towel, Eve grabbed onto his jacket and slid down onto the road. Kyle heard his voice yelling towards the phone on the dashboard as if he was listening to someone far away, "Michelle, she's bleeding! There's blood everywhere! Help me! What do I do?"

The mother from the car next door was there within seconds. "I've got her. You pick up the phone." She lay Eve down on the white lines of the road between their cars and put a jersey under her head. A ring of fascinated and helpless faces grew around them as people got out of their cars to come look.

Kyle's hands shook so badly that he knocked the phone to the floor. He picked it up from next to the unopened packet of pacifiers that was lying in the footwell, a last-minute purchase in the hope of quiet nights once the baby came. Now he hoped his baby screamed the whole damn highway down. He couldn't think about the alternative.

Michelle started talking again. Her voice on speakerphone was the only sound around them. "You need to keep her lying flat and calm. I've raised the priority of the ambulance call. They've said they'll drive up the other side of the motorway against traffic. There's only self-drivers making it through on that side anyway. You need to ask someone to wave them down."

A man stepped forward from the circle of voyeurs, "I'll do it."

Kyle tried to say thank you but the words wouldn't come out. The man clapped a hand on his shoulder. "It'll be OK," he said and then made his way across the lanes of stopped traffic to stand on the median barrier waiting.

Kyle hunched forward over Eve and held her. The mother sitting next to her gently took the phone off him. He could hear her answering Michelle's questions. "Her eyes are open but she isn't responding to me. Her breathing is really shallow. There's a pool of blood on the ground. It's hard to tell how much."

He couldn't look away from his sheet-white pale wife. He realised he hadn't heard her screaming for several minutes, and that scared him more than the screams had. The wind blew the smell of idling exhausts across his face and chips of gravel from the grey road dug into his knees. It wasn't supposed to be like this. They'd toured the hospital a month ago in preparation. It was smooth and white and smelled of antiseptic and visitor's flowers. This highway wasn't part of the birth plan.

He didn't even notice the sound of the ambulance siren coming closer until a paramedic took the woman's place across from him.

"You need to move aside for a moment please sir, so we can get her on the stretcher. What's her name?"

"Eve."

"Eve, you need to hang in there just a bit longer. We've got you. Can you hear me? Eve?" The paramedic was shaking her shoulder gently as she spoke.

Kyle stumbled after them as they loaded her into the ambulance. He sat across from her in the back, watching the paramedic working fast. He didn't have a lot of experience with paramedics, but he knew desperation when he saw it.

A voice came from the front, "The rig wants to do a U-turn and go through the 'burbs Robyn. This side is starting to clear and we've got human drivers heading towards us."

"We don't have time. Hit the override and tell dispatch to get the police and those SDCs to clear us a lane. If they can save their owners' lives, they can damn well help the rest of us plebs too," the paramedic replied.

Kyle was dimly aware of the flashing red beacons of the self-drive cars playing across Eve's face as the ambulance sped past them in the opposite direction at high speed. The ten-minute drive took five thanks to the entire route being cleared ahead of them simultaneously. He would have been impressed if he wasn't so worried that it was five minutes too long.

They rushed Eve off to theatre as soon as they arrived and Kyle was left sitting in a waiting room. The same thought kept playing over and over through his mind. If only they'd bought the new car he would be holding his baby in his arms right now.

Eve had rolled her eyes when he'd said no to buying one. She'd told him they were lucky they had the option, that they had a responsibility to use their privilege to be early adopters and help bring the price down for everyone else. He'd laughed at her and told her shopping was not a social service. He didn't need his savings to be on the front-lines of a technology revolution.

The fan in the corner had something stuck in the revolving blades and it made a rhythmic clicking noise as it wafted air across Kyle's face, cooling the tracks of his tears until they felt like glaciers creeping down his cheeks. He put his head in his hands and he waited.

INDENTURE IS A NERVOUS SYSTEM

First published in *Worlds* from Black Hare Press in June 2019

When the snowflakes fell in dull-red flurries, we marvelled at their colour. When they melted, they made rivulets across the cracked, barren landscape like arteries running across the planet's skin.

The sunlight didn't glint so brightly off the floating habitats above us now that they had succumbed to the rust that was colouring our snow. The shine was wearing off our relationship with the people looking down uncaring at our suffering as well.

Rust makes some metals stronger. They relied on us miners to know which ones. When the structures came crashing down, blood-red rivulets ran across the planet's skin.

THE GIFT OF TIME

First published in *New Orbit Magazine* in November 2019

Ella paused as they left the house, touching the flaking paint on the doorframe. It was theirs now. She caught herself smiling a little and stopped before Mark noticed.

There was no way they could have afforded this place themselves, even as run down as it was. Anyone who didn't own a house when the cure went mainstream was the same.

As they walked back to the car, Ella adjusted the itching waistband of the black skirt she'd found for the funeral. Even though it was too tight around her pregnant belly, it still managed to constantly slip down and expose her skin to the cool breeze and Mark's family's sideways glances.

Ella was not yet welcome in Mark's world. It had taken her years to find a man she could love who would be able to provide for a child. By the time she met Mark her biological clock was ticking, the second hand slowly losing time. The result was a whirlwind romance and a shotgun wedding.

Mark's mother had died before Ella met him. Today, they had farewelled his father after a tragic work accident. His family all knew they would inherit the house. The judging looks they gave her at the funeral suggested they wouldn't put it past her to have arranged the accident just to get it. She had been desperate for stability, but not that desperate.

Owning a house with only a tiny mortgage put a whole different spin on her impending motherhood. The Government had finally legislated to allow employees to limit their work to an 80-hour week. Ella had thought they would both be stuck working far more. Their baby would have joined all the others in the 24/7 childcare centres and week-day boarding schools that had sprung up everywhere ten years ago. Now they had options. With an 80-hour week she could work at night and be home for most of their child's waking hours.

Mark opened the car door for her and she wrapped an arm around his shoulders and squeezed a little before she got in, kissing his cheek. He didn't respond. His red-rimmed eyes were staring into the distance at the street where he had grown up.

◉

Mark was remembering a childhood spent out in the street here with his friends, biking in endless circles until his parents called him in for dinner. They weren't that far from their apartment, only 10 minutes' drive, but this street was a different world. Fenced stand-alone houses were screened by mature trees that draped their branches over the road. This little cul-de-sac was immune to the frenetic pace of the nearby city.

The calm was broken as they pulled out onto the busy road. Mark tapped his fingers on his armrest as they sat waiting to merge, begrudging valuable time lost. It was one of their generation's great ironies that time was so much scarcer now that they had more access to it.

"I might talk to my work about taking a little longer off and dropping my hours after the baby comes. I think we can probably afford it now," Ella said into the silence of the car.

"Jesus Ella. Could you give me just one day to be sad? Is that too much to bloody ask? I'm not talking about this now," Mark replied.

He rubbed his red eyes and turned away from her for the rest of the short trip. When they got to their carpark, he slammed the door as he got out. "I'm going for a walk."

He was gone two hours and returned to an apartment in chaos – half-packed boxes everywhere he looked. His hands clenched into shaking fists by his sides and he opened his mouth to yell. Ella instinctively put her hands on her belly. He looked down at her trembling fingers frowning and then stalked into their bedroom without another word, slamming the door behind him.

The argument continued for the next two weeks in the few hours each day that they had together. Routine interactions became coded messages of hurt or attack. The tension never left their little apartment.

On the bad days, Mark told her she was irrational and hormonal, that she would see sense once the baby arrived. Everyone else worked hard. Why did she think she was so special? Sometimes he even managed to sound sympathetic.

On the calm days, Mark pointed out how much better off they would be if she went back to work. How would they pay for their child's treatment if they didn't start saving now? She wanted the best for their child, didn't she?

Deep down Ella knew he was right. If they couldn't afford the cure for their baby, he would only be able to work 12 hours a day. University would take two or three times as long. He would struggle to find a decent job and afford to live. Any woman who wanted children would steer clear of a relationship with him. Ella had broken up with the love of her life because he hadn't had the treatment and couldn't afford it any time soon. How could she expect any different for their son? If they saved their money, maybe she could even have another baby one day. She'd never let herself dream that could be possible.

Ella was tired of arguing. She sighed and felt their baby shift inside her. The sharp point of an elbow or knee was visible through a shirt that was fast becoming too small. She rubbed that little point gently, feeling tears form in her eyes. She had waited so long. She wanted to be with this baby so much. It wasn't fair.

Ella's own parents had been able to stay home with her. If she thought back hard, she could remember days of baking muffins at home with flour flying everywhere or playing 'the ground is lava' in the playground.

She wished the damn sleep cure had never been invented. It was supposed to liberate them and give everyone more time to have fun and do the things they loved. Instead, just like when women entered the workforce 100 years ago, all it did was tempt and then trap people into a cycle of working more and more. Back then, it meant families needed two incomes every week. Now it meant they needed 200 hours of income every week. Her tears fell faster and faster and great wracking sobs shook her body.

Mark sat down beside her and wrapped his arms around her, placing a hand on the alien protrusion moving across her skin. He bent his head down to rest on hers. It was the most contact they'd had in months.

Ella leaned back against him and breathed in the unique combination of smells that was her husband.

As they sat like that, Ella cried out and clung tight to Mark's hand. A wave of tension and pain built across her stomach and then slowly subsided. When she could move again, she tilted her head up and looked at Mark with wide eyes. "I think this is it. I think the baby's coming!"

It was the next day before they finally met their child for the first time. Before that, were long hours of Mark helplessly watching Ella's pain. Eighteen hours after that first contraction, the midwife spoke from the end of the bed. "It's a beautiful boy. Do you want to cut the cord, Mark? It's a little short for mom to have her first cuddle."

Mark hesitated as he cut the cord under the midwife's instructions. He let her arrange his hands so he was holding the baby properly. His arms were stiff with nerves as he carried the baby, his son, around the bed.

Ella's face was drawn and pale. "Can you hold him for me Mark? I think I might drop him."

He gingerly squeezed himself onto the narrow hospital bed next to her. Once their baby was safely nestled between them he could finally relax. He looked sideways at his wife with dawning understanding. Deep down, if he was truthful, he had thought she was being weak and desperate. Somehow, he had never noticed how strong she was, what she could endure. The moment was broken by a demanding series of rhythmic screeches from their son.

The midwife helped Ella to feed their baby for the first time and peace descended on the room as he fell asleep wrapped in his parents' arms. Mark stared down at the red, scrunched-up little face of the person they had made together. It was a long time since he had slept himself. He wondered what filled a newborn's dreams and what they had really given up when they'd left their own behind.

A GALACTIC SYMPHONY

First published in *Apocalypse* from Black Hare Press
in December 2019

At the tipping point when bio-domes became mass-producible, we spread across the galaxy consuming each planet until it was exhausted.

We left a trail of abandoned cities. The bio-domes collapsed first and then everything else succumbed. Eventually, all that would remain were the giant pipes that had fed the dome and carried away our waste.

Each pipe jutting from the ground was a different length and width. The native winds would blow across their open mouths in mournful harmony.

When we finally ran out of worlds we turned back in desperation. All that remained was the symphony we had wrought.

RETOUCHED

Not previously published.

It was 9:23 when Basil's 9 am appointment finally knocked on the studio door. Basil was standing right next to it, but he listened to the tick of the second hand from his watch for a full minute before he opened the door. He thought about leaving it another minute for good measure.

Standing before him was a woman in her late twenties or early thirties with long brown hair tied up in a messy ponytail. Basil hid his disappointment as he shook her hand. She wasn't wearing any make-up and she looked exhausted; not exactly the advertisement for his skills that he was hoping for.

"Welcome, I'm Basil. You must be Laura," he said.

Laura smiled. "Nice to meet you. I'm so sorry I'm late. I was trying to put my baby down for his nap before I came. He must have known I had somewhere to be!"

Basil assured her he totally understood while he resisted the urge to check the time on his watch again. He showed Laura where he needed her to stand and gave her a coffee before beginning the process of adjusting the lights and heights to fit her perfectly.

"How old is your baby? Is he your first?" Basil asked as he worked. He wasn't particularly interested in the answers, but he knew he needed to build rapport with her or the whole shoot would just be awkward.

"Yes, he's my first. He's four months old and I'm pretty sure I've been awake non-stop for most of them."

"I don't know how you do it. You look amazing," he said. He kept up the string of praise until he was sure he had something he could work with.

"I'll be in touch soon with the photo," he said as he showed her out. "I'll make a few little tweaks here and there, just to make sure it really pops."

Basil had barely cleared the coffee cups away when the next appointment knocked on the door, right on time. Ryan was a realtor in his forties. His eyes wandered around the studio assessing its value as he spoke. He spent a lot of time describing each house he'd sold in the last year and how he'd tricked the purchasers into offering more than it was worth, or the vendors into accepting less.

Basil started to wonder if he really wanted to work with realtors after all. He had never taken a dislike to someone so quickly. Still, if he managed to catch the glint of shark in this man's eyes then perhaps the hidden message in the photo would act as a warning for Ryan's future clients.

"I'll be in touch soon with the photo," Basil said once again when they were finished.

"You will edit it won't you?" Ryan asked. "I have an image to maintain you know." His hand was rubbing his middle-aged paunch as he spoke.

Basil resisted the urge to sigh. "Of course," was all he said.

When his last appointment arrived, it was like someone had adjusted the aperture on his day and let all the light in. Victoria was everything Ryan was not and what Laura hadn't yet grown to become. Her 60-something years hung heavier on her face than was fair, but her voice and her eyes were still bright with an energy that Basil imagined she must have had since her youth.

They spoke a long time before the shoot and even longer afterwards. Basil found himself unburdening all his worries about his livelihood to Victoria's sympathetic ears. In turn, he listened to her concern that she and her husband had nothing in common now that they had retired. She seemed relieved to be able to speak freely, away from the oppressive silence that was thickening at her house. They reluctantly bid each other farewell as the room grew dark that evening.

Basil stayed up late that night to edit the photos with a strong black coffee by his side. The smells of slightly burnt beans drifted up to his nose promising a bitter kick. He turned on his new computer and selected a single photo from each of the shoots that captured something unique in his subjects.

The computer had come pre-loaded with advanced photo-editing software from its previous owner; that was one of the reasons Basil had paid more than he could afford for it. The software was like nothing he had ever seen. The interface was so smooth he felt euphoric as he worked.

Under his ministrations each of the photos was refined to match Basil's image of his subjects' perfect selves. The dark circles faded away from Laura's eyes. The tiny marks of stress were smoothed away. The messy ponytail was messy no longer. She looked bright and full of energy. The essence of motherhood minus all the hard bits.

Ryan's photo lost the middle-aged paunch he was so worried about. The wrinkles on his forehead and the lines by his eyes and mouth disappeared. He adjusted the eye-shape infinitesimally to give him just a hint of the sinister personality that Basil had glimpsed; it was his small warning to the world.

Finally, Victoria. Most of the wrinkles disappeared like the others, although he left some signs of the years of laughter and tears that made her so compassionate. He should have stopped there, but Basil couldn't help himself. He wanted her photo to look the way her conversation made him feel. He sculpted the lines of her face like a painter, gently shifting the boundaries. Puffiness disappeared and sagging skin was taught once more. He was careful to keep the changes slight, hoping she wouldn't notice exactly what had been done and would only see that he had revealed her true, beautiful self.

Basil looked down at his watch – 4:45 am. He rubbed his eyes and looked with surprise at the cold cup of untouched coffee beside him. He emailed the three photos to their subjects and crawled into bed exhausted.

A loud banging on his studio door woke Basil up. He grabbed his cell phone from the table next to him and stared at it, rubbing his eyes repeatedly. It said it was Sunday, 11 am. He had missed eight calls. Saturday seemed to have disappeared, he wasn't sure where. The banging on his door started again.

Basil pulled on some jeans and a shirt and staggered towards the studio door. "I'm coming!" he called out. When he opened the door, Victoria was standing before him. Her eyes were red and swollen with tears.

"I need your help," she said.

He made them both coffee and they sat in his lounge instead of the hard chairs in the studio. Basil waited for her to start speaking, but she just sat staring down into her mug.

"What can I do for you?" he finally asked.

Victoria swallowed and her eyes flicked up to his face and then back down to her mug. "I need you to talk to my husband. He thinks I lied about you being a photographer and that you must have been a plastic surgeon. My face is… different." She reached up to touch her cheek. Now that Basil was more awake he could see something had changed. She looked a little younger, her beauty showing through a little more than it used to.

"Have you had something done? Yesterday maybe? You do look different," he said.

"No! Of course not! My husband won't believe me. He thinks I've been hiding money away to get it done. He told me to leave and not come back till I'm ready to tell the truth. Even my children think I'm lying. They… they told me I must have done something because I look so much prettier. Did they think I was ugly before?" Victoria started to cry again, her shoulders shaking with suppressed sobs.

Basil hesitated and then reached out to put an arm around the distraught woman sitting on his couch. "You have never been ugly Victoria. You are beautiful. I could see that when you first walked into my studio." She turned her face into his shoulder, still crying. Basil wrapped his other arm around her, holding her tight. He was surprised at how angry he was at her family. How could you do that to someone you love?

Victoria lifted her face off his shoulder and looked him in the eyes. "What happened to me?" she whispered.

Basil reached up to touch the skin on her cheek without thinking. He traced the line of her cheekbone that was more defined than it had been for 20 years. A sick feeling started in his stomach and his heart beat faster. He had traced this exact line with his mouse last night, no, the night before.

He opened his mouth to utter an impossibility, but before he could get the words out Victoria's lips were touching his. Basil froze in surprise; his heart beating faster for a different reason now. She started to pull away but he shifted his hand behind her head instinctively and pulled her back.

Victoria stayed that night, and the next. She didn't tell her family where she was. They had pushed, she had fallen.

Basil woke up early on Tuesday morning and got up without disturbing the woman in his bed. He looked down at her sleeping face and the impossibility he had banished from his mind returned. She looked ageless, a little too perfect. She looked retouched.

He made himself coffee quietly in the kitchen. His exaggerated stealth made him feel like an intruder in his own house. The noise of the jug boiling, the cupboards opening and closing, the slight clink of a teaspoon taken from the drawer. These were all things that might wake his guest and he needed time to think, time to clear his head.

He sat down with the coffee and the morning's newspaper, postponing the thought he was so carefully avoiding. The front page was taken up with a photo of the mangled wreckage of a car wrapped around a lamppost. He started reading the article –

Local woman Laura Berkley is in critical condition in the hospital after a late-night supermarket trip went wrong when the new mother fell asleep at the wheel. An eye-witness reports that Ms Berkley was heard repeating "I didn't feel tired." as she was taken to the ambulance by stretcher. An anonymous source has suggested the woman may have been awake for more than 70 hours at the time of the accident and was behaving unusually. Police are awaiting blood test results to identify if drugs or alcohol may have been a contributing factor.

He looked up from the paper and stared into space. It couldn't be related. It was impossible. Poor tired Laura.

Basil's phone started vibrating on the table. He answered the call on the second ring and shut the door to the lounge before he started speaking.

"Hello?" he said.

"Basil. It's Ryan Craig, realtor."

Basil's heart skipped a beat.

"Uh, hi Ryan."

"I wanted to say I'm very happy with the way the photo came out. I've updated all my advertising material."

Basil relaxed a little. "Great, I'm glad you like it. If you wouldn't mind putting the word out for me I'd really appreciate it. You know how it is."

"Well, yes. About that. I wonder if it might be better for me to be your exclusive realtor customer. Give us that edge of difference you know? Keep it unique."

Basil frowned and his lips tightened. "That's… not really what I had in mind."

"We should meet to discuss the details. This could be a great partnership. I was thinking we could do another shoot. Maybe a bit sportier. You can use your little tweaks to really show the muscles."

Basil tried to swallow the lump that had suddenly become lodged in his throat.

"Sorry Ryan, I'm all booked up this week. I'll give you a call when I have some space." He hung up without waiting for a response. His hands shook a little as he turned his phone off and walked over to his studio to stare at the computer sitting innocently on his desk. He couldn't avoid it any longer.

He turned the computer on and looked at the three folders in 'Clients'. He opened Ryan's first. The final photo was still the same, retouched tummy staring flatly back at him. He checked the original as well. If anything,

Ryan looked slightly fatter than he remembered. His complexion looked ruddier, as if he'd been out on a week-long bender.

He opened Laura's next. The youthful energy glowing out of her face in the final photo was a sad irony given the circumstances she now faced. His mouse paused on the original file for a long moment. He shook his head at his own folly, opened it and then sat staring at the screen unblinking. Laura's eyes were sunken into deep dark circles edged in red. Her face was a sickly grey. It was not the face he had photographed. He was starting to panic.

He almost couldn't bring himself to open Victoria's photo. The retouched photo was unchanged of course. After 10 minutes he managed to open the original. He sat with the two images before him on the screen – before and after, original and retouched, natural and supernatural. He started to relax at first. There was no physical degeneration, no grey face staring back. But then he looked closer and saw the slightest of changes. She looked sadder somehow. Something about the energy that had shown through in her eyes had faded.

He was concentrating so intently that he didn't notice Victoria approaching until he heard the gasp of her indrawn breath over his shoulder.

"What did you do to me?" she asked.

He turned to face her, to explain. He saw the same pain and betrayal in her eyes as when he had opened his door to her two days ago. Only this time it was directed at him.

The whole story came out in the lounge. He told her about Laura and Ryan. He told her he didn't understand it, that he hadn't meant it to happen, that he couldn't believe it was possible. He told her he had never meant to hurt her.

"What did you mean to do then, Basil?" she asked. Basil wasn't used to dealing with a relationship like theirs. He should have heard the warning, but he didn't.

"I meant to show your beauty to the world. To make the photo perfect." His voice was earnest, but as he said the words they felt wrong.

"You thought I looked old and tired and no-one would like the photo if it looked like that too. You thought your image of me was right and beautiful and the real me is wrong and ugly. You thought you had the right to make me look just how you wanted. And worse than that, you thought I would be grateful for it." Her words were coming faster and faster. She had betrayed her family for this man who had told her she was beautiful.

Victoria stormed back into the studio. Basil was a few seconds too late behind her as she right-clicked the retouched image and hit delete. She slammed the mouse so hard that he thought he heard it groan a little in response. Then she just stood there with her back to him, shoulders shaking with her sobs.

He reached out to her, not sure what to say. She pushed his arm away. As she turned to leave, he caught sight of her face. It was the same face that he had seen last Friday – old and sagging and full of character. Or almost the same anyway. She had lost something in the intervening days. He called out to her as she walked away, but she was done with him.

Two days later, Basil went to visit Laura in hospital, computer in hand. He had thought long and hard about what Victoria had said and he had made two realisations. Firstly, that what had happened was both incomprehensible and truly wrong. Secondly, having finally understood the effect of unilaterally changing someone's appearance, that he needed his clients' permission to undo what he had wrought.

He paused in the doorway to the hospital room. Laura's husband was in the process of leaving, holding their baby out to her. She winced in pain as she kissed his forehead. The medical paraphernalia – casts and traction and drip – all combined to make even that small motion almost impossible.

Basil nodded to the man as he left, and then entered the room to stand by the bed. "Hi Laura, thanks for seeing me," he said.

"Hi." Laura hardly looked up as she spoke, intent on twisting the sheets between her fingers.

Basil pushed on. "I need to talk to you about the photo I sent you. It's going to sound crazy, but I need you to listen to the end. Could you please listen?"

Laura shifted in discomfort on the bed. "Why not? I'm not going anywhere."

Basil told her about Victoria, glossing over their affair, and he told her about Ryan's calls. "I think when I took the signs of tiredness away from your face, maybe you couldn't feel tiredness physically anymore even though it was still affecting you. Maybe that's why you didn't realise what might happen."

Laura lay staring at him with dead eyes. "What you're saying is impossible. My accident was my fault. I have to live with that forever."

Basil heard the guilt in her voice that he had caused. The guilt he could probably never take away. "Look – could I please just delete the retouched photo from my computer? If it really is impossible, it won't make any difference to you. Please. I just want your permission."

"Do what you like. I can't look at that photo now anyway. I won't look like that ever again."

It wasn't the kind of consent he'd been hoping for, but it was enough, wasn't it? He opened his computer before she could change her mind. He looked again at the original photo of her. It personified extremes of human exhaustion he hadn't even thought possible, much worse than two days ago. She looked gaunt and emaciated. He needed to fix this. He right-clicked the retouched photo, pausing over the delete button for a long second.

Click.

Alarms by the bed started shrieking. Basil could hear footsteps running down the hallway towards him, many footsteps. Laura looked like someone had punctured her soul and let the life leak out of her body. Her eyes had sunken deep into her face, which was tilted to the side not breathing.

The door crashed open and he stared at the doctors running into the room in stunned disbelief.

"What happened?" one asked him, voice urgent.

But all Basil could do was shake his head in despair. A nurse charged in with a defibrillator. Basil was unceremoniously pushed from the room.

It was days before Basil could do anything but lie in his bed, staring at the wall. He couldn't bring himself to call the hospital or Laura. It was only the fact that he had unfinished business that got his body moving again.

He turned on the computer with shaking hands and opened the original photo of Ryan. He was noticeably larger. His jacket was stretching at the seams and the buttons were popping. His neck was slowly and inexorably succumbing to a wave of flesh.

Basil picked up his phone and called Ryan. "We need to talk."

"Have you rethought my proposal? I can come in this afternoon," Ryan said

"No, it's not that. You need to understand. This thing that's happened. It's not right. It's dangerous. Someone might have died already. We need to change you back before it's too late. I'm going to delete your photo."

"No! You can't! I won't allow it."

"I have to," Basil's voice was pleading. He needed this to be over. But what if Ryan didn't give him permission and something terrible happened again? He wanted so badly to just delete the photo, but he couldn't make himself do it.

"We can work this out Basil. You'll see. I'll come over now." Ryan hung up the phone.

Basil sat in front of the computer in his studio. He held his head in his hands, fingers gripping tight to his hair. He was still sitting like that when Ryan's knock sounded at the door.

Basil kept sitting. He knew Ryan would never agree to delete the photo.

The knock came again.

Basil's head stayed in his hands. What was the point?

In the otherwise silent room, Basil could hear the ticking of the second hand of his watch next to his ear like a time bomb waiting to go off.

The door splintered and crashed inwards. Ryan strode into the room with a sinister glint in his eyes and a gun in his hand. He pointed the gun at Basil.

"You will take another photo of me. You will take away all the fat this time and give me muscles. You will make my jaw look stronger. You will take the grey from my hair. And then you'll give me the computer."

Basil stared at him in horror.

"Do you think I won't use this? Get your camera. Now!"

Basil thought of the warning he had left in the photo; the way he had made Ryan look just a little bit evil. He looked at the gun pointed at his head and he went and got his camera.

When he returned, Ryan started stripping off in front of him.

"What are you doing?!" Basil asked in alarm.

"I don't want just my face fixed. I want all of me fixed. Get a mirror so my whole body can be in shot."

Basil's mouth dropped open and he stood swaying slightly.

Ryan pointed the gun at the ground and pulled the trigger. Shockwaves of sound reverberated around Basil's panicking mind and he ran for a mirror.

It didn't take long to take the photo. This was a utilitarian picture, no art here. Basil sat down at the computer to edit it. Ryan held the gun to his head only an arm's length away. The barrel filled Basil's peripheral vision.

Ryan hadn't even bothered to get dressed. Basil wasn't sure whether that or the gun was more distracting. He fought down a hysterical giggle. He had barely begun editing when the orders started.

"Not like that, I want it bigger."

"My arms don't match, you need to even them up."

"Take that mole off my leg."

Basil's shaking hands fell down to his sides. He turned slightly towards the cold silver metal that was now pressing against his head as Ryan leaned in.

"I can't do this with you watching over my shoulder. I'm an artist. You need to trust me. You can tell me what you want changed once I've finished the first take," Basil said.

Ryan's eyes narrowed. "Fine. I will watch you instead of the screen. But if I think you're doing anything dodgy, I will shoot you. Understand?"

Basil swallowed and nodded.

Ryan pulled a chair up to sit opposite the photographer. "Oh, and Basil?" he said.

"What?"

"Make my dick bigger too while you're at it."

Basil tried to ignore Ryan and the gun. He tried to pretend he was alone like usual, just an ordinary photography job. An ordinary job literally recreating someone's genitalia while they watched.

When he was far enough through that he thought Ryan wouldn't notice, Basil removed the hint of malignance from the realtor's eyes. He waited a few more minutes and then deleted the first retouched photo and the original of the photo he was editing. He was hoping he could undo some of Ryan's insanity. He resisted the urge to look up and check if anything had changed as he continued to work. Ryan started tapping the gun on his leg. "Can't you hurry up?" he said. Nothing had changed.

The retouching was almost complete, but Basil had come to a decision. He couldn't allow this to continue. He had caused too much pain already. What if his actions meant Ryan killed someone in his madness? What if he'd made evil Ryan live forever?

Before he could rethink, Basil deleted the retouched photo. Ryan yelled in alarm and Basil heard the gun go off for the second time that day. Only this time it was followed by a pressure in his leg. He looked down in surprise as the blood starting to bubble out of his thigh like some sort of primordial mud pool.

He felt rather than saw Ryan lunge forward and crash into him. Through the ringing in his ears, he heard an anguished yell—"No!" Was that him or

Ryan? He saw the gun lifting up again. His hand was still on the mouse. The original photo was open on the screen. He acted on ridiculous instinct alone. His fingers clicked delete as the barrel of the gun became parallel to the ground, perpendicular to his face.

He closed his eyes tight against the inevitable. He wondered if he would hear the bullet that killed him or if sound travelled more slowly than the ending of consciousness. He inhaled once, and then again. Eventually, he realised the bullet wasn't coming. He opened his eyes and looked to his right. There was no sign that Ryan had ever been there, if you ignored the gun on the ground and the blood still oozing from the hole in his leg.

Basil limped to his wardrobe and tucked the computer out of sight. He didn't want it anywhere near him, but he couldn't get rid of it. Anything could happen to Victoria or Laura if he did; if they were even still alive. Then he called an ambulance.

Forty years later, Basil was no longer living in the studio. He had never taken another photograph after that day with Ryan. He'd moved to an apartment in town and taken up accounting, a nice safe occupation. The computer was tucked away in a purpose-built safe, locked behind a painting on his wall—a Victorian portrait of a young man. He worried about what would happen to the computer when he was gone.

His hands had become translucent with age and his breath was rasping in his lungs. He wondered if there was an afterlife. When he was young he'd been sure there wasn't, but that was before. Maybe there was an afterlife. He thought about those days forty years ago and wondered how his soul would be judged if there was. He wasn't sure if his heart started fluttering and racing in panic or because it was finally giving up on him.

The doctors had told him he didn't have much longer. He had lied and said he wanted to be home with family. He had no family, only pain. He levered himself out of his armchair and slowly limped across the room. He stood in front of the painting on the wall so long that his old legs started trembling underneath him and small spots of light started floating across his vision. The ticking clock filled the silences between his laboured breaths.

He imagined the young man in the portrait giving him a sly smile as he reached out to shift it aside and open the safe.

THE GENESIS OF INTERDIMENSIONAL TRAVEL

Not previously published.

On the periphery, of the edge, of the boundary
of the meniscus that contains all the matter of our
universe
is an endless something pushing nowhere.
It couldn't be pushing somewhere
because it contains everything.

And so it must be pulling everywhere.
Pushing nowhere
while pulling everywhere
is a lonely place to be.

What if it takes a wrong turn?
It might inadvertently end up somewhere.
And there's no one to ask directions from.
What it needs is a way to connect
with other somethings just like it.

Alt-ernate – Melanie Harding-Shaw

We're all just looking for a place to belong.
So it reaches out and something else,
exactly like it but slightly different,
pokes back.

Melding surface tensions stretch to form invisible
pathways.
Infinite crossroads of connection.
#Spacebook: a multiverse social network.

THE SIX STAGES OF REVENGE

First published in *Trickster's Treats* in 2019.

He was merciless.

Drip.

When I first saw him looming over me, I felt sorry for him. I could see his soul's fire within him, and it was just the acrid smoke from a spent match. He had no flame left and nothing much there to start with.

In the flickering light, none of the gathered audience saw the grease stains on his sleeves nor the broken veins in his cheeks. No one was looking at him anyway. Their eyes were all on me. They'd paid to bear witness to a spectacle and if they looked away for too long, they might miss it.

Drip.

Still, there was plenty of time. I wasn't really dying again. He wouldn't let me. I was making him money. It would be fine. I'd find a way through this setback, just like I'd found my way through so many others. It was probably all just a dream, anyway. Any moment now, I'd wake up on the cold floor upstairs with a head-pounding hangover.

Drip, drip.

That gave me a fright. I jumped. The crowd gasped, sucking the air from the room. They burst into applause. I was fading. I struggled to breathe. He laughed at the near-miss. Laughed.

Fury burned hot within me. How dare he laugh? What kind of a man has the power to save a dying soul, only to put it in a flame for amusement? A candle flame, no less—fragile and transient. The wax that was fuelling my remaining life-force burning lower and lower, until I flickered out. Life, corporeal or not, shouldn't be a parlour trick. I knew the answer to my question, though. The same kind of man who'd killed me in the first place.

Drip, drip.

My anger made the wax melt faster. I couldn't look down to see how much longer I had. Couldn't remember how high above the table I'd been to start with. Maybe, if I entertained them well enough, they'd give me more fuel to feed on? A new wick and wax to let me live longer?

So, I danced for them. I changed my colours to a hundred different hues of fire. Contorted myself into shapes no natural flame could take. I watched the still shadows of the crowd on the walls and the surging light around them from my antics.

The crowd stared on, entranced. The concrete basement underneath the dingy bar was only furnished with a single wooden table. I knew I had a body when

I'd entered the bar, but everything before the man and his knife was hazy. Had I danced up there, too? Had these same people watched me there?

Drip, drip.

The faces of the crowd loomed higher as my wick burnt down. They were not going to save me. I was dying again and this time there would be no reprieve. Could flames cry? Would I extinguish myself if I tried? I stilled my motion. Lapsed back to my smallest self, nestled in a tiny oasis of melted wax. The dripping liquid was the closest thing I had to tears.

How many times had he done this? How many desperate flames burned down before his eyes? Did these people even know what they were watching?

The crowd began to turn away, but he still watched. His eyes traced my every flicker. His frown grew deeper as people left the tip jar empty. I had cut the show too short. Stopped entertaining them too soon.

Drip.

I was near the end and there was nothing I could do. I was dying. If I could have closed my eyes I would have, but a flame has no eyes. We were all alone, then. His face would be the last thing I'd see. I thought I had a few more minutes, but he had other ideas. He reached out to pinch me dead. I watched his hand grow near.

Screw denial. Screw anger, bargaining, and depression. Screw acceptance, even. I was beyond all that. I was nothing but fiery wrath.

His sleeve draped above me. His old, greasy sleeve.

Grease burns really well.

Drip.

I was merciless.

RADIO SILENCE

First published in *Frozen Wavelets* in September 2020.

They targeted our communications systems every time. You'd think we would have learned.

They took our voices first.

The world fell silent, but we continued typing messages to each other on our phones.

So, they took our eyes.

The world was darkness, but sound came back as we turned to audio messages. Eight billion generic virtual assistant voices conversing.

So, they sent a sonic bomb that took our hearing.

With only touch remaining, the scientists felt their way around their labs, programming robots to undertake delicate surgeries to create a direct brain-to-brain neural network.

What did they expect would happen?

A FAIRY TALE

First published in *NewMyths* in March 2020.

The light from the hallway shining through Michaela's open door was just enough for someone with very acute vision and lots of practice to read a note to the tooth fairy. Everyone who lived in the house was fast asleep, even little Toby in the bassinet in his parents' room.

The quiet of the night was broken by the whirring of tiny wings on two figures flying across the room. They would have looked a lot like winged snakes if it weren't for their clawed arms and legs and human-like heads. Blue-green iridescent beetle-like chitin covered their entire bodies. Their ears twitched independently from each other, listening for any approaching danger. An extra carapace of smooth chitin capped their heads, almost like a very slick bob hairdo. The carapace was ready to extend down over their face and ears at a moment's notice to protect them from attack or the dissolving acids of human saliva.

Sascha had tagged along with her mom that night to help keep watch. They didn't travel together often, but now that it was just the two of them they didn't have much choice. It was too dangerous for Elowen to give birth alone. Sascha had been about the same size as her mum for six months now but her carapace still hadn't fully grown. She couldn't get the tight seal needed to enter a human mouth. She would be the last of her litter to mature. Her older brothers and sisters were too busy with their own lives now to rub it in.

Elowen was here for Toby but her eye had been caught by the glint of light reflecting off a gold coin in the darkness of Michaela's room. Mother and daughter read the note by the bed together. *Dear tooth fairy, I lost my tooth on the way to school. Please can you find it for me? Love, Michaela.* Generations of dedication to perpetuating that tradition amongst the humans was still working in some households at least.

Elowen let out a chattering moan, her tail thrashing. "Sascha! It must be about to hatch. We have to find it!"

Sascha looked at her mom and tried to push down the sickening anxiety rising within her. Elowen's thrashing had started an undulating motion underneath her skin. Sascha shook her head. "You're too far along. You need to lay those eggs now or you'll lose them."

Her voice was agitated. It was stressful enough when they needed to launch a rescue mission for one of her younger siblings. Why did it have to be the one night in the last five years that her mom was ready to lay? Not to mention that it was last time she would ever lay. She wished her dad were still here, but wishing couldn't bring him back.

"We'll never be able to search that big a space if you wait for me to finish laying. Go get started and I'll come find you when I'm done," Elowen said.

They stared at each other for a long moment. Laying was a very risky business. You needed at least one other fairy there to keep watch and run interference when the humans started putting things in their screaming child's mouth. Even without that, you sometimes needed help getting a mouth open to escape when you were done.

"Mom, you can't. I'll stay with you and we'll search together afterwards. We can't put all those eggs inside you at risk for one child. Please. Don't ask me to go." She didn't say what she was really thinking—that she couldn't face losing her mom too.

Elowen shook her head. "Your brother or sister could be lying alone on the side of the road right now about to be eaten, or stood on, or drowned by rain. Go!" Elowen's teeth were bared now, rows of sharp points promising a fight if her daughter didn't do as she said.

Sascha looked down at her feet. "If you're not there in the next two hours, I'm coming back to find you," she said.

"Don't stop searching till you find it," Elowen replied. Then she launched herself into flight towards Toby's bassinet in the other room.

Sascha didn't waste any more time. She knew her mom would calm down once the drive to lay her eggs had left her, but until then she wasn't likely to see sense. She made her way out into the cold breezy night and cursed the clouds that made it that much harder to see the ground.

As she left the house, she heard a wail from Toby as Elowen stabbed her clawed feet deep into his gums to plant the first egg. She imagined her mom's delicate ears assaulted by the sound echoing around the child's mouth. Her wings would be tucked tight to her back leaving only her clawed hands and feet to cling to her perches and avoid being swallowed. She would have lowered her head carapace before she entered, moving by feel alone in the darkness so the saliva couldn't drown her or damage her eyes.

Sascha was filled with fierce pride and fear for her mom and for the day in the not-too-distant future when she might be ready to lay her own first eggs. Even if her mom got herself out when she was finished, her wings would be wet and useless for many hours. She could easily be crushed by Toby while she was helpless. Sascha needed to find the missing tooth fast and get back to her.

She flew back and forth in a grid pattern along the footpath. Her multi-faceted eyes swung pendulum-like along the ground, searching for any hint of reflection that might reveal the ripe chrysalis of her sibling. She was careful to keep high enough above the ground that any cats or dogs wandering in the night would not be able to catch her in their jaws.

As each hour passed, Sascha fought to ignore the growing despair inside her. A hint of red was leaching into the sky when she finally caught a glimpse of white in the green verge. She could see tiny hairline cracks forming along the hard shell, but she didn't have time to check any further. She grasped the chrysalis in the claws of her feet and launched herself back towards Toby's house and her mom.

The house was silent despite the rising sun. Its occupants were exhausted from a trying night. Sascha laid the chrysalis down on the floor behind a bedside table gently so as not to crack open the shell. Then she flew to Toby's bassinet and perched on its edge searching frantically for any signs of her mom.

Elowen was nowhere obvious, which left two options. Either she was underneath him or she was still inside his mouth. Sascha wasn't supposed to venture into a human mouth until her carapace was fully grown, but if her mom was still inside the boy then she could be swallowed at any moment if Toby rolled over. She had to get her out.

Sascha launched herself off the side of the bassinet and landed on Toby's rosy cheek. The breaths from the boy's nose rustled her wings as she folded them on her back. The trick was to try and get him to open his mouth without waking him up and drawing an adult's attention. She started by running her claws gently over Toby's lips. His mouth twitched a little and then Sascha had to leap into the air to avoid being swatted by the sleeping child's hand.

Next, she tried tickling under his nose. This time she was braced ready to jump clear, but she almost got sucked up a nostril by a sharp intake of breath and then she was blown end over end by his sneeze. As the world spun around her, Sascha desperately twisted her body towards Toby and saw a sliver of her mom's iridescent green body inside the boy's mouth.

She landed on the bed, all too conscious of the light starting to creep in around the curtains. There was nothing for it. She'd tried subtle. She was going to have to be more direct. Speed would be everything. She landed on the child's cheek once more and before she could second-guess herself, she stabbed a clawed foot deep into Toby's lip. He woke with a screeching howl. Sascha fought to tug her claw free. She tucked and rolled into the boy's mouth just as his hand slapped onto the pinprick of blood welling up from his lip.

She was momentarily disorientated by the cacophony of sound around her. It vibrated her brain and teeth until she felt like they might rattle out of her head. It was only the sight of her mom lying unconscious wedged inside the boy's mouth that got her moving. She fought her way along the gums where neat rows of lumpy eggs now lay buried. They were a promise of many annoying younger siblings in her future, if they lived long enough to collect them in the coming years.

The child's tongue was vibrating high in his mouth with his screams. As the gaps between his wails grew longer, his tongue started falling down towards her. Her eyes were already stinging from the saliva she couldn't shield herself from. Sascha stabbed her foot into the child's mouth once more in desperation, and almost fainted from the crescendo of noise that resulted. Then she scooped her mom up in her arms and staggered along the bucking, slippery, red pathway as fast as she could towards freedom.

They tumbled out of Toby's mouth and into the blankets just as Anna came to scoop him up and take him to her bed. "Hush, Toby. It's OK. It's sleepy time. Please go back to sleep." Her eyes were barely open or she couldn't possibly have missed spying the two fairies lying in the blankets.

Sascha peeled her mom's head cape back from her face and saw with relief that she was still breathing. The saliva had started to seep in under the seal and she could see one eyelid was red and weeping with acid burns. Her wings were stuck together on her back as if glued. Only time would tell if they would dry out properly and become usable again.

Sascha closed her foot claws gently around her mom's wrists and started climbing hand over hand up the mesh sides of the bassinet. In a night of terrible luck that mesh was a small blessing; without it she wasn't sure she could have got her mom out. She felt her joints pulling and straining with the effort of carrying her, but she couldn't let go. Her head was spinning and her vision was starting to blur as she reached the top. Somehow, she managed to lever Elowen over the railing, but the weight of her body was too much. Rather than drop her, Sascha let go of the bassinet and they fell entwined together to the ground. They landed with a crack near the small white chrysalis she had left tucked safely behind the table on the floor.

Sascha groaned in pain, feeling the bruises and damage forming to the soft tissues under her exoskeleton. Thankfully, the skeleton itself wasn't cracked. With the last of her strength she dragged herself and her mom behind the table with the chrysalis.

They lay like that all day—Elowen unconscious and Sascha in a daze. She couldn't risk moving in the daylight even if she'd been able to carry both her mom and the chrysalis with her bruised body. She forced herself not to think about what would happen if they couldn't get home.

When darkness fell again, the chrysalis started to crack open between them. Sascha roused herself from her stupor enough to reach out and pull a piece of white calcification off her brother's face. She felt someone else's hand on hers as she touched the baby fairy. Her mom was finally awake. Their glittering eyes met in the darkness and they smiled.

"Your dad would be so proud," Elowen whispered.

LOVE CAGE

First published in *Takahē* in April 2020.

Marie sits in bed and stares down at his sleeping face. She brushes a lock of hair from his eyes and flinches when he stirs. He rolls onto his back and begins to snore. Her shaking fingers trace the metal by his heart. A perfect silver circle chamber – machined by the others and fused into his skin just like everyone else's – it contains all the love ever gifted to him. Her other hand strokes her own silver circle over and over again.

Her fingers pause at the depression that will pop his chamber open. They are not meant to be opened. Her fingers press down gently on the cool metal and she stares entranced at the sparkling fireflies of her love for him. She only pulls back when her tears start dripping down onto his chest.

She lies back on the bed and opens her own chamber. Unlike his, the metal is warm on her fingers. She has to use her phone's camera to see down into the depths that continue past where her body ends. She sees a maelstrom of glowing black currents. Her tears turn to retches as she finally feels the sickening swirling mess of his love inside her.

She looks again at his chamber, not bothering to close her own in the hope some of his love might fall out. It's a fruitless hope though because it sticks like tar to all it touches.

She watches a bright firefly of her love hit the cold wall of his metal and fizzle into acrid smoke. More and more of them throw themselves against the cylinder's walls until a thick plume of smoke is drifting up to the ceiling from his chest. The last single bright spark drifts from his chamber to land just inside the lip of hers. She gently closes the lid to keep it safe.

She slips out of bed, careful not to disturb him, and shoves as much she can carry into a pillowcase. In the hallway, she glances in the mirror at the black bruise spreading from her eye. She can still feel that last tiny bright spark fluttering inside her chest, pushing back the darkness. She holds her head high as she walks out the door.

THE ENEMY WITHIN

Not previously published.

You can't beat me on a good day but on that day, I was vulnerable. I stared at the creepy anthropomorphic hand that was somehow still intact, the stump of its wrist crunched down into the cracked brick paving where it had plummeted to the ground. It looked like a giant with too many faces had been buried in front of the City Gallery and was fighting to claw its way back out of the ground. Like some kind of bizarre zombie emerging from its grave to terrorise the Wellington CBD. A crowd gathered, flat white coffees in hand, to shake their heads.

No-one was injured that time, but I wondered how long that would last. The attacks had been spreading across the city like a rot and I was powerless to stop them because I never saw who was responsible. If I thought about it any longer, my panic would overwhelm me. I turned my attention away from the scene of my failure and towards the nearby ocean.

Staring out across my harbour, Te Whanganui-a-Tara, had always calmed me. It was as if my frustration, my darkness, followed in the path of

Ngake out to Cook Strait. On that day though, it didn't work. All I could see was the snapped water-whirler sculpture on the waterfront. An empty platform of accusation. Another failure. Another piece of destruction taunting me.

Away from the sea then. I would take my darkness into the energy of the city, let my people buoy me up. Across the rainbow crossing painted against the dark tar seal of prejudice. Past the drifting sounds of buskers, some delighting and some desperate. I paused at the colourful fountain to watch the anticipation on the faces that surrounded me as they waited for the water to crash down from the slowly filling buckets.

The sounds of splashing water blended with children's squeals of delight, but all I saw was the leftover scum from an attempt to fill its base with bubbles. Was that another act of destruction? Subtler and more insidious. Designed to catch me off guard and leave me crying tears in some vain attempt to wash the dirty water away. No-one will notice a little extra salt.

I knew that I should find a place that gives me joy. I would not find my attacker with a broken spirit. My power comes from wind and creativity, from welcome and belonging. I knew that laneways hung with twinkling fairy lights would do more for me than drifting down broken alleyways and treasured buildings closed for earthquake repairs. I knew that I should watch the people gathered to weave harakeke flax together on the grass and not the beehive's politicians somehow scoring points from pointless games.

Sometimes, knowing is not enough. Sometimes, trying is not enough. Sometimes you ascend Mount Victoria and spin in place surrounded by 360 degrees of beautiful vista and still you cannot forget this place is also called Matairangi and Tangi Te Keo and it was once a place of mourning.

My sadness swirled around me as gusts of air that pushed my people away. From that vantage point, I saw a hint of shadow forming below. The next attack. I was angry, then. My winds gathered at my back, screaming down the hillside. Whoever thought they could threaten me, vandalise me, break me, did not know what they faced. My howling gales flew before me, targeting the darkness. I could feel it fleeing, running scared. The sky was my friend and the bitterly cold southerly was my strength. It would not escape.

My blasting attack forced the shadow to Karori, Kaharore, to my snares. I felt the darkness drop into Zealandia, trapped within fences anchored in my earth to keep such predators away. I concentrated myself in that place, searching to find who it was. I could feel its taint all around me, sense its creeping tendrils straining to break free.

I looked down into the waters of the entrance lake and I saw it, finally. I saw the shadow.

It was my reflection.

The shadow was me.

My winds stopped and silence fell. The surface of the lake grew still. Even the takahē paused in their step, one foot raised, sensing that they should not make a sound. I felt true despair then. The rot I could not protect my people from was me.

My earth shook in tremors and my tears fell as a deluge from the sky. I felt parts of me crumble into the harbour. I felt valleys fill with water until they spilled out to the sea. I pulled away, hoping the shadow would stay snared, but still it followed me.

Maybe I was broken. Maybe that was all I was. Maybe I should shake and keep shaking until it all crumbled. Every last bit. And then I would be nothing and I would be free. A flash of shadow sprung up in my harbour and I despaired. Even those precious waters were not immune. I poised to break everything in two but before I could, the shadow spat at me.

For a second, anger shot through my sadness. How dare my despair spit at me? And then I saw the people gathering and I looked closer. A single whale was swimming in my waters, paying me no attention whatsoever. And all along the water's edge my people stood sharing their delight with each other despite the rain. I read, again, Patricia Grace's words on the writer's walk beside them and I remembered that my people loved me. My people understood me. Maybe I could be more than the darkness, more than what is broken.

I am Te Whanganui-a-Tara. I am Wellington, Pōneke, and Wellywood. I am hills, wind and glistening harbour. I am creativity and coffee; culture and cable car. I will not let anything destroy me. Not even me.

TEPID

First published on Twitter in September 2018.

She had bright red lipstick, heirloom silver, and a 1950's pinafore. In a house of perfection, the tepid tea was a warning ignored. You are not welcome. If you stay long enough to finish it, you will never leave.

Melanie Harding-Shaw
@MelHardingShaw

She had bright red lipstick, heirloom silver, and a 1950's pinafore. In a house of perfection, the #tepid tea was a warning ignored. You are not welcome. If you stay long enough to finish it, you will never leave. #vss365

5:40 PM · Sep 26, 2018 · Twitter Web Client

AN EYE FOR AN EYE

First published in *Frozen Wavelets* in February 2020.

The air was thick with the metallic tang of blood, singed flesh, and sweet yeast from the sparkling wine. Members of the emperor's court filled the room with polite laughter and snide comments. Their brightly coloured silk robes in stark contrast to the plain black cotton of the soon-to-be-initiated. Five years of training and the biggest gamble of Gwen's life were about to play out. There was no way to know whether tonight would mark her final revenge, or a lifetime of abject slavery.

One by one, the black-robed initiates were allocated their fate—puppeteer or puppet. All sworn to dedicate themselves solely to the emperor's entertainment. At last, only the two of them were left. Of course, it had come down to this. The whole city knew the story of Gwen's family's fall from grace. How it had been carefully orchestrated by the parents of Belle, who stood by her side dressed in the same black robes. No-one had been able to prove it, though. Until now.

The shame of that day years before had driven Gwen's mother to take her own life. Gwen had been sold to the emperor's private puppet theatre to cover the family's debt. Not like Belle. Belle had volunteered for the honour. She had been certain that her family's favour would see her initiated as a puppeteer; certain Gwen's life as a puppet would be one more chance to twist the knife into her family's back.

Gwen bowed low as the emperor approached. She searched his face for any sign that he had read the evidence she'd given him at their private audience last night; any sign that her machinations would see her through. He gave nothing away. His face so still that not one of his thirteen dangling earrings swayed.

In his hands, he held the puppet-master brand. The smell of singed skin was stronger now, and the brand only just hot enough for one last use. Puppets were marked in other ways. Gwen saw Belle look over at her and smirk. They both dropped to their knees in unison and shut their eyes to await their initiation as tradition dictated.

Gwen drew in a shaking breath, and then another. The gasp of the crowd sounded seconds before burning pain seared down her cheek. Her tearful eyes flew open as the brand drew away, leaving her face scarred from temple to chin. Her heart soared in grim vengeance. She had won. Belle's ragged sob sounded from next to her as strong arms held her down.

"No! You can't do this to me!"

Belle's cries grew louder with each steel ring that pierced her arms and legs to hold the marionette strings. Her screams twisted with those of her watching mother in strange harmony as they dug the eyes from her skull and pressed in cold glass spheres. The gasps of the crowd turned to stunned silence as they processed what had happened.

Gwen looked down at Belle's face. She could just make out the single green button suspended in each glass eyeball before her eyelids swelled closed over them.

"Why?" Belle's father groaned from the spot where he had collapsed on the floor nearby.

The emperor smiled. "Their lives are mine alone to play with."

WHEN SUPERMARKETS GO BAD

First published in *Breach Zine* in March 2019.

The old woman
Wrinkled in body and soul
Motherhood faded to a distant memory
Observes the child screaming in the supermarket while
his mother stands by
And she judges.

The mother
Flushed in shame and frustration
Sleep faded to a distant memory
Wishes she and her child could be transported
elsewhere, anywhere alone
And she despairs.

The child
Tear-stained in panic and confusion
Calm faded to a distant memory
Struggles to contain the emotions bursting from within
him, torn from his chest
And he howls.

Alt-ernate – Melanie Harding-Shaw

The supermarket
Cold-blooded in desire and calculation
Insentience faded to a distant memory
Feels the pounding of tiny hands on its skin, the
despair and the judging
And it feeds.

A SECOND CHANCE

First published in *Midnight Echo* from the
Australasian Horror Writers Association in November
2020.

I crouched to pick up the single yellow and white
thread from the dirt on the side of the road. I held it
close to my nose to inhale its scent, half expecting it to
smell of the lemons printed on the apron's fabric. But,
of course, it did not. It smelled of scared child and
dust burning on an overheated radiator.

I placed the thread on my tongue and swallowed it.
It did nothing to fill the hole that she had left. It tasted
of broken dreams and the vanilla ice cream that had
dripped down her fingers before she could eat it.

The road ran across the landscape like a ribbon
inexpertly sewn around the hem of a pinafore,
bunching in places where the road workers could not
be bothered taming the rolling dunes. They liked the
idea of the road but lacked the patience to follow
through. I had lacked patience when sewing the apron,
but only to ensure that her little fingers could more
easily drop a trail of threads for me to follow.

Alt-ernate – Melanie Harding-Shaw

My footprints stretched behind me in the red clay. On the days when a squall moved in with bursts of rain, the earth's pigment leached into the water and each drop became a splash of blood on the remains of my trail. Squalling weather, squalling child. Some days it felt like I really was bleeding out. Those were the days of harsh sunlight and the sandpaper of rubbing the crystallised salt of my sweat from my face.

Until the soles of my shoes gave out. Then I bled for real.

I feel every thread I've found writhing in my belly. Does she have butterflies in her tummy as she senses me growing closer? I have their larvae. The acid of my stomach will liquefy them, and I will be a walking chrysalis, a living icon of rebirth, of a thousand rebirths. Perhaps in one, I will find her.

Only, I am no longer walking. There are no more threads to find. The trail is gone and so is my heart.

I am lying gasping for air on the road. There is a shadow in the distance. I like to think it is the car in which she flees. It gives me comfort to think she is close at the end. I would have been a good mother to the child. She could have been mine.

The writhing has changed now. My back arches against the rough gravel and my mouth stretches wide. I have drawn my last breath. As the darkness sets in, my final exhalation swirls from deep inside me, a swarm of lemon cotton butterflies bursting past my jaws to freedom.

A little girl sits on the side of the road as her mother fills the radiator with shaking hands, one eye always on the road behind them.

"Mama, look," she says. On her finger perches a single yellow pinafore butterfly.

By the time her mother turns, it has already disappeared inside her mouth.

MOTHER CEPHALOPODA

Not previously published

I call you Mother.
Your voice sung through our membranes in the deep.
The sound of water rushing from your body past your
children,
A percussive counterpoint of life-giving oxygen.

They call you Smothers-Above-Water.
Your pigments shifted as you climbed their ships.
Silent and invisible as your body wrapped around our
enemies.
A singular executor of ruthless assassination.

You call me 28965.
You will not live to see me earn a name.
I watch you sink, gaunt and haggard, to the ocean
floor—starved.
One last sacrifice for the cause.

We call you hero.
You are a cold stone statue in the empty city of our
people.
Three tentacles raised—one for each wound taken in
the fight.
But no symbol for your final battle.

I call myself nothing.
Your memory is not comfort, but pain.
Your memorial, a symbol of progress stymied in
pursuit of war.
I will not swim that path.

SYNAESTHETE

First published in *Black Dogs, Black Tales* from
Things in the Well Press
Reprinted in *Year's Best Hardcore Horror Volume 6*

The first time I remember noticing a flash in someone's eyes was the day I started preschool. The shadow of black and red in the teacher's eyes matched the feathers lining the korowai cloak of the girl sitting next to her who was leaving that day to start school. I thought that was clever. The flashes had always been there, of course. In the eyes of my parents and the adults who came to visit. When I was old enough to wonder, I thought they must be spirit animals. Guardians, perhaps. I was oblivious in the way that many children are. Or maybe I just didn't want to see.

I can remember the first time I looked in the mirror to search my own out. Staring into the depths of my eyes and feeling a moment of panic that there was nothing there before I saw the shadowed outline, the hint of movement from the rise and fall of its breath. I shouted at the mirror to try and wake it, but it did not stir. I sometimes wonder what would have happened if I had succeeded in waking it that day. It was only when

I closed my eyes and saw the afterimage on my eyelids that I could make out the shape. A hound as black as my pupils curled in sleep. It wasn't until puberty hit that I started to realise the truth.

○

Scotty was the first boy I thought I wanted to kiss. I didn't tell anyone because all the girls wanted to kiss him and it was ridiculous to think he might pick me. I just stared at the back of his head in class. Admired the casual swagger that somehow came across even when he was sitting still.

And then the party. Those first gulps of cheap and burning vodka. Stumbling into a bedroom, and there he was. His casual swagger, now a stagger. His hands pulling me closer. The sudden sickening realisation that I did not want *this*.

I pushed him away in panic. "No!"

"I've seen the way you look at me," he slurred.

I shook my head, and stepped back.

"Freak."

My stomach churned with dread and my frantic eyes met his, searching for a sign that this would not make my life "over". That I would be able to show my face at school on Monday. The thing is, I didn't usually meet people's eyes. Somewhere between kindergarten and that party, I had realised no-one else saw the flashes and I had decided I would not see them either. I watched their mouths instead: the twitch of hidden amusement at one corner or the downturned edges of lost patience. Maybe I would have been prepared if I had been watching eyes all those years. If I had let myself accustom to my changing sight.

I stared into Scotty's eyes and I saw the rabid peacock tearing at his brain. Clawed feet scratching gouges down his amygdala as its sharp beak wrenched at optic nerves stretched so tight his eyes might pop out the back of their sockets. The bird's majestic iridescent wings spread wide, bloodstained and razor sharp as they beat within his skull, slicing the soft tissues like the cutty grasses that used to catch our unwary arms as we walked to the beach.

I stood in that room and I screamed and I did not stop screaming until the ambulance came. I could not show my face at school that Monday or any Monday after.

It was weeks before I could even step foot outside my room. Weeks before I could bring myself to cry on my mother's shoulder. I watched her mouth as I crept out into the lounge. I saw her fear for me in the tightness of her lips. I heard the tentative tremor in her voice, the uncertainty that she might say the wrong thing and make it worse. I kept my eyes down, scared of the coloured flashes lurking higher.

I sat beside her and leaned my head on her shoulder. I felt the comforting weight of her arm around me. I couldn't see her face from there. I was safe.

"I love you," she whispered.

I didn't say anything. I could feel a tendril creeping down my face, caressing me. Each time it pulled away, I felt pinpoints of my cheek stretch outwards one by one. Tiny circles of pain. Not a tendril, but a tentacle. I jerked upright to stare at her, despite knowing better. I didn't notice the metallic reflections of the octopus's eyes within hers at first. I was too distracted by its tentacles tearing off the features of her face to shove them into its beak. I could see glimpses of her flesh further in. Pieces of her nose and ears being ground down by a tongue covered in rows of teeth.

I tore myself away and ran back to my room, the sound of her voice calling after me muffled by the squelching of those tentacles rending her faceless.

I could feel a sickening movement in my eyes, the first stirrings of a slumbering animal. I broke every mirror in the house.

My therapist thought that writing might give me an outlet, and it did. I chatted to other writers online. I could communicate, be supportive, and have value; and I did not have to see their faces. As I grew more confident, I could even meet them sometimes. I would sit and stare down at my paper, focussing only on the letters I was forming on the page. I would laugh at their jokes, offer solace for their trials. But, it is a hard thing to look away from the pain in a friend's voice.

There came a day when I lost focus. I glanced up for a moment as I spoke.

"You are doing it! You are a writer already!" I tried to say.

My words were cut short by a missile smashing into my nose. I covered my face in my hands, but not before I saw my friend's eyes bulging outwards with the pressure of a thousand cuckoo's eggs. The mother bird invisible inside their skull but for the sound of her beak clacking in sinister pleasure. I staggered to my feet as a stream of projectiles flew at me, beating me backwards. I caught a glimpse of my friend as I ran away. Unimaginable pressure sending eggs erupting from their scalp like pumice flying from flesh volcanoes. Their red blood lava oozing from the open wounds.

The squeaking sound of hound's teeth worrying at my synapses, not unlike the noise of biting into haloumi, echoed in my mind and drove me running home.

So, I locked myself away from the world once more, reaching out only through my keyboard and the screen. Groceries delivered to my door. Feet dragging, shoulders hunched, and the smell of loneliness permeating every space. The ache of claws and teeth inside my skull never left me and I wondered if there was anything left there and what that hound would feast on once it was stripped bare. There was a single mirror in my subsidised apartment. I had covered it with rainbow lines of duct tape. The colours made me feel like it was a choice; an interior design quirk that I could remove any time I wanted. I never did.

You can't stay inside forever, though. The day I met Sid, I was walking to the letterbox. She was walking her dog, a golden terrier. Even with my eyes cast down, I noticed her nails reflecting in the sun. They were the most beautiful nails I'd ever seen; works of art with rainbow chrome colours shifting as she walked. I didn't know it then, but people often stared at Sid. She didn't match what they expected to see. She didn't match who they expected her to be.

I stared at Sid, too, and maybe she saw the horror in my eyes because she looked away. Her shoulders hunched slightly against the blow she thought might come, just like mine. Everyone I met had something eating away at them. Sid was different, though. The thing consuming her was not inside her skull like mine. Its human mouth was latched onto her legs gnawing on an Achilles tendon while the weight of its body dragged behind her each step she took. As I watched, its jaws loosened but only so that its rooster talons could tear chunks from her calves. It was the cruel alpha, driving her away. A monster denying her the right to live.

Somehow, she strode on despite the creature hanging off her that was part human, part beast and all the cruelty of the world. I watched her pained footsteps almost pass my gate and I couldn't take it anymore.

"Hi," I cried out, and she turned around, uncertain. I could feel the gnawing in my own brain pause.

"Hi," she said.

I stood and stared at this beautiful woman, the horror of her parasite now hidden behind her legs. I tried to imagine how to convey to her that I was different, too. I didn't have the words. I reached up and buried my face in my hands. My dank, unwashed hair fell forward to hide my face as sobs shook my body.

She didn't see my dirty nails clawing into my eyes, tearing out the creature I could feel inside. And I am certain she did not see the black hound that I threw to the ground between us. Its teeth were bared in a snarl and its muscles were poised to leap back up; to savage my face before digging a hole back into my brain as if my frontal lobe was freshly mown grass begging for its claws.

She saw the red scratches down my cheeks, though. She saw the tears. She reached out to me, a stranger, and she hugged me in the street.

"Do you want to come for a walk?" she asked.
I nodded.

There is a forest at the end of my street where I had never ventured. At the entrance was a sign: "Dogs must be kept on a leash."

Sid saw me reading it. "It's to protect the birds, our taonga. We can't let dogs roam free or they will destroy them," she said.

Sid set off towards the trees. I looked at the black hound stalking beside me. I could still see the vestiges of my brain tissues on his snout, my blood colouring his whiskers. Then I looked at the almost human creature ahead of me, clinging to Sid's shoes. It had lost its grip when I started walking beside her, shrunk back a little. It was still horrifying, but now it was no bigger than the playful terrier trotting by her side.

I glared at the black dog, looked deep into his eyes. We can't let dogs roam free or they will destroy what is precious to us. I bared my teeth and planted both feet firmly on the track. His snarl faltered, his ears pressed down to his skull, and his tail twitched downwards until it was pressed tightly up under his belly.

I pointed at Sid's creature and he streaked towards it, slamming his head into its side and sending it careening into the shadows of the undergrowth where it peered at us cowering. When he returned to me, I reached down to touch him with a trembling hand, to finally feel that coarse black fur. He tried to snap at my fingers, to crunch the tiny bones in his powerful jaws. I slapped his nose and grabbed the leash lying across his back. I had never even noticed it was there.

"Are you coming?" Sid asked from up ahead, her steps now gloriously unconstrained.

"Yes."

She smiled at me. I could tell because of the tiny creases forming by her eyes. In their glossy depths, I could just make out the reflection of the silver fronds of a young ponga fern beside the track.

SEE ME

First published in *National Flash Fiction Day*
MicroMadness finalists in June 2019

Long hair reminds you of clutching seaweed. I shave.
You linger near every rose. I tattoo myself with a floral
army. Still, you do not see me.

You do not see me when I carve your likeness from
trees that grow beneath my touch.

Nor notice when I shape the water running down
your drain into letters of desire.

I lock my carvings away. Arm myself in tatters of
despair. Accept I'm more floral creep than rose.

You see me then. Walk me to the ocean. We
discover where my words washed to, and float
together on tides of missives.

ACKNOWLEDGEMENTS

Huge thanks to everyone who has helped me on my writing journey over the last five years! This is going to be a long list, sorry.

Thank you to my husband for reading my first short story and telling me he thought it was a worthy entry to the genre ('These Walls' still hasn't been published but it's out on submission again so I haven't included it here). Thank you to my children for their patience, pride and excitement, and to the rest of my family for their support even when they think my stories are weird lol.

Thank you to my 'book club', Becca, Natalie and Emily, who listened and encouraged throughout the drafting of my first novel and still do so.

Thank you to all the people who have read my stories, given me feedback, nominated me for awards, written a review, or reached out to say something kind about my writing. You have no idea what a difference it makes.

Special thanks to the amazing communities of writers I have found and created, and to the many unexpectedly awesome friendships that resulted. I have learned so much from you and you pick me up and keep me going every time I falter. There are so many that I am bound to miss someone, but I'm going to try anyway.

To the writing friends who reached out to me on Twitter and gave me hugs, company and support when I turned up terrified to my first NatCon, thank you! (Looking at you Janna Ruth, M. Darusha Wehm, Andi C. Buchanan, Octavia Cade, A.J. Fitzwater, Marie Hodgkinson, and Cassie Hart).

To my Speculative Collective slack crew, I would be a mess without you. I am grateful for you every day (shout out to T. and Cassie for making that group happen with me and for being ridiculously talented writers and friends).

To my Wellington Speculative Creatives drinks group, thank you for turning up month after month and reminding me I'm not alone.

To my Witchy Fiction indie publishing team, you helped get me through lockdown and were the only reason I wrote much at all in 2020. You folks are awesome (everyone go buy all the feel-good kiwi witchy fiction novellas at witchyfiction.com!).

To Amber and Marie, you brought the joy back to my reading and writing and you're the best team of cheerleaders I could ever hope for.

To the many other writers who have also made the time to teach and support me, thank you, including:

Graci Kim, Toni Wi, Casey Lucas, Isa Pearl Ritchie, Ryn Yee, the Brilliants, Pippa Werry and the Wellington NZSA branch committee, the Hugo Award finalists of 2020 who I worked with, and the Codexians. And especially to:

- Sarah Pinsker, my SFWA mentor who probably doesn't even realise how much she helped to put my brain and my writing career back together when they broke in 2020.
- Cassie Hart, who became my partner-in-inclusion and a dear friend in the lead up to ConZealand and who I am so ridiculously proud of. You have taught me so much, you are a constant inspiration and you are always there when I need you.
- Andi C. Buchanan, who has generously and endlessly given me advice and feedback on far more than just my short fiction.
- M. Darusha Wehm, who has consistently given me some of the best advice I've had on short fiction and writing as a career, starting when they had just won a Sir Julius Vogel Award and I was hiding in the corner of the bar and most recently also at a bar where they told me that of course I could put a short story collection out in three weeks just because it would make me happy. I promise we don't only communicate at bars.

And my eternal thanks to everyone who has published my stories, including the publications in which many of the stories in this collection have appeared:

Apocalypse from Black Hare Press, for publishing 'A Squash of Commuters' and 'A Galactic Symphony'

The Arcanist for publishing 'Strands of Our Tomorrows'

The Best of British Fantasy 2019 from Newcon Press for reprinting 'The Fisher'

Black Dogs, Black Tales from Things in the Well Press, for publishing 'Synaesthete'

Breach Zine for publishing 'A Devoted Husband' and 'When Supermarkets Go Bad'

Curses & Cauldrons from Blood Song Books, for publishing 'She Was No Witch', 'Green is More Than Skin Deep', and 'Break Glass in Case of Emergency'

Daily Science Fiction, for publishing 'A New Cold War'

Frozen Wavelets, for publishing 'Radio Silence' and 'An Eye for an Eye'

GeyserCon Book for publishing 'An Avian Introduction'

Little Blue Marble, for publishing 'GAC ATG ATT ACC'

Midnight Echo, for publishing 'A Second Chance'

New Orbit, for publishing 'Revolutions' and 'The Gift of Time'

NewMyths, for publishing 'Unrequited Sonata' and 'A Fairy Tale'

newsroom, for publishing 'The Fisher'

NFFD Micromadness, for publishing 'Big Brother' and 'See Me'

Takahē, for publishing 'Love Note', 'Only Child', and 'Love Cage'

Trickster's Treats from Things in the Well Press, for publishing 'The Six Stages of Revenge'

Wild Musette Journal, for publishing 'Common Denominator'

Worlds from Black Hare Press, for publishing 'Indenture is a Nervous System'

Year's Best Aotearoa New Zealand Science Fiction and Fantasy Volumes 1 and 2 from Paper Road Press for reprinting 'Common Denominator' and 'The Fisher'

Year's Best Hardcore Horror Volume 6 from Red Room Press for reprinting 'Synaesthete'

ABOUT THE AUTHOR

Melanie Harding-Shaw is a speculative fiction writer, policy geek, and mother-of-three from Wellington, New Zealand. Her short fiction has appeared in numerous publications, including Strange Horizons, Daily Science Fiction and *The Best of British Fantasy 2019*. She won the Sir Julius Vogel Award for Services to Science Fiction, Fantasy and Horror in 2020.

Sign up for her newsletter on her website to be notified of new releases.

You can find her at:
www.MelanieHardingShaw.com
Facebook @MelanieHardingShawWriter
Twitter @MelHardingShaw